Robert Vaughan

Memoir of Robert Alfred Vaughan

SALZWASSER
VERLAG

Robert Vaughan

Memoir of Robert Alfred Vaughan

Reprint of the original, first published in 1864.

1st Edition 2022 | ISBN: 978-3-75259-251-1

Verlag (Publisher): Salzwasser Verlag GmbH, Zeilweg 44, 60439 Frankfurt, Deutschland
Vertretungsberechtigt (Authorized to represent): E. Roepke, Zeilweg 44, 60439 Frankfurt, Deutschland
Druck (Print): Books on Demand GmbH, In de Tarpen 42, 22848 Norderstedt, Deutschland

MEMOIR

OF

ROBERT ALFRED VAUGHAN,

AUTHOR OF

"HOURS WITH THE MYSTICS," &c.

BY

ROBERT VAUGHAN, D.D.

SECOND EDITION,

London and Cambridge:

1864.

Alfred Vaughan.

ADVERTISEMENT.

A BRIEF Memoir of Robert Alfred Vaughan was published with the two volumes of his Essays in 1858. Many persons have expressed a wish to see that Memoir in a separate form. It is reprinted in the present volume with some supplementary matter, and additional letters. It has been thought that the story of a life so rich in promise, and, we may add, in performance, may be placed with advantage in the hands of intelligent youth, and that it may not be without its lessons to the early manhood of the thoughtful.

March 5, 1864.

CONTENTS.

MEMOIR.

CHAPTER I.

SCHOOL AND COLLEGE LIFE.

1823—1846.

IN times of peace, said the Greek orator, sons bury their fathers; in time of war, the fathers bury their sons. Some men know that this inverted order of events may take place from causes with which war has nothing to do. In nature, the young plant is sometimes seen to droop and die, while the old is spared. Decay and death are appearances which appeal to our tenderest sensibilities wherever they come, doubly so when they thus come. But it would not be well that it should be otherwise. Our early days are visionary enough as it is, what would they be if sickness and the grave came only to the well stricken in years—to those worn down with the labour and care of a long pilgrimage? Providence, moreover, is often admonishing us that there is as little to secure us against such visitations in eminent goodness, or in the highest capacity for doing good, as in the fond dreaming of our youth. The young man's strength, and the wise man's wisdom, have their uses, but we are none of us left to account our own strength, or our own wisdom, as necessary to the course of human affairs. The world did without us once—it will do without us again.

It was not, I suppose, unnatural for me to have thought, that should anything in my own somewhat laborious life be deemed worthy of a record, the hand now cold and still, but which had so often guided the pen at my suggestion, would have been the hand to perform that piece of service. But the Supreme Will has not so determined. It is left to the father to tell the story of the son, and to do what may be done toward rendering a life once so rich in promise, but which has proved so brief, as influential as may be.

The will which seems in this instance to be not according to the order of nature, must always be the expression of justice, wisdom, and goodness. Let God be true!

Robert Alfred Vaughan was born in Worcester, on the 18th of March, in the year 1823. His birth on that day was two months earlier than had been expected. It is probable that this circumstance had its effect on his future constitution. During the first year of infancy his health was good. Subsequently he became sickly. Through the next two or three years his friends had much reason for anxiety on his account. But after that time he gradually gained strength. He never became robust, either in bone or flesh, but he improved greatly in appearance, was much admired during his years of boyhood for a certain mixture of masculine and feminine beauty which then distinguished him, and was capable of taking his full share in work or play with those of his own age.

In 1825 myself and family removed to Kensington. My residence in Kensington and at Notting-hill extended to the year 1843. During those years my son continued under my own roof. My aim in relation to him was to combine as far as possible the advantages of home education with those of a public school. It was not easy to realise that object. Alfred was my eldest child, and the only son spared to me beyond infancy. Until thirteen years of age his training was under my own superintendence, generally along with one or two pupils, a little older than himself, as companions. By this arrangement he was not left to be wholly dependent for society either on persons much beyond his own age, or on his sisters, who, besides being of the other sex, were all his juniors.

With this course of proceeding I had reason to be satisfied. Of all the blessings that may befal us in childhood, there cannot be a greater than that of a home where there is discipline, but a discipline without fear. It was always a solicitude with me that my own household should be one of that description. The family is the State in little. The effects of a reign of terror are the same in both. Deceit and falsehood seem to become legitimate weapons when left as the only means wherewith the weak can hope to oppose themselves successfully to the lawlessness of the strong. How far the kindly influences of home contributed to form the future character of my son it is hardly for me to say. But in that circle he grew up, evincing a disposition to reverence whatever was proper to be revered, and to love whatever was proper to be loved. It was pleasant also to me to observe, that with his never-failing amiableness of temper, the firmer elements of his nature seemed to be getting deeper root, and to be acquiring greater strength. The room for fear concerning him lay chiefly in this direction. The man wanting in firmness may not perpetrate great mischiefs, but he will always be in danger of conniving at them. His sins of omission will be as great and as disastrous, probably, as the sins of commission in the case of men whose natures have been cast in a different mould. My son early saw the importance of guarding against danger in this form, and his fixedness in principle and feeling grew with his growth.

When he had reached the close of his thirteenth year, there was room to believe that he might be safely left to make his way with those of his own age. He entered the school of University College, London, possessing a knowledge of Latin, Greek, and Mathematics creditable to him for his years, and with a measure of culture and of general information unusual at his age. His love of reading, especially on literary subjects, was early manifested. While quite a child, he often sat at my feet for considerable intervals, with his book on his knee, he intent on his work, and I intent on mine. On one of those occasions I remember him suddenly looking up and saying, "Papa, I think I *must* be a literary man." "Do you, Al," was my reply; "what makes you think so?" "Because," said he, "I remember being within the sound of the scratching of your pen almost as long as I can remember anything."

Before entering University College School, Alfred had attended more than one course of my lectures as Professor of History in that College. His favourite reading thus early was in history and biography. But he never allowed himself to be diverted unduly from the studies which modern opinion has placed at the foundation of a liberal education. The following extract from a letter with which I have been favoured by one of my son's earliest friends, furnishes some information concerning his school-days :—

"I must go back to my schoolboy days to recal my earliest remembrance of your son, for whom I then first contracted that regard which I ever entertained for him. He entered the school of the University College, London, after I had been there a short time. Well do I remember him as he appeared on the first day of his entrance, standing on the stairs, leaning back against the banisters, amidst the crowd of waiting boys, with his large head and long curls, and frock coat, an object of universal schoolboy observation, and therefore derision, blushing deeply at the rude remarks, and striving to avoid the tormenting jeers that rose up around him on every side, and with singular good humour, I must say, did he then, as always, bear the jests and teasing to which he was subjected. We soon, however, learned to respect and like him. He was a diligent scholar, and even then fuller of knowledge, and fonder of its acquisition, than most around him. I well remember the lively interest he used to show in many of our daily lessons—in the Greek history classes especially—and the witness which his translations, compositions, and *viva voce* answers in the class bore to a careful preparation at home. He evinced, too, in all our classical lessons, a real taste, and an enjoyment and appreciation of the books read, almost incomprehensible to his companions generally. I remember this fact particularly in reference to *Herodotus*. It was thus he first won my admiration and respect. I mention these facts, because they serve to mark some of the leading traits of his mind, his disposition to constant and careful study, and his natural love of literature—a love, I believe, which constantly increased.

"At the University College I saw a good deal of him, and there I learned still more highly to value him, not only for those traits of character already mentioned, but also for his pleasant geniality of disposition, and that appreciation of the humorous which is so attractive always in a man of true dignity and strength of character. He was, perhaps, too reserved and retiring by nature to be universally popular or generally social; but all who knew and understood him esteemed him as a man, and prized his friendship and sought his society for the real enjoyment (neither mean nor profitless) that it afforded them. Besides a manly dignity of character, that naturally carried weight with it, he possessed an intellectual life and activity that would have promised fruits of industry and culture in one endowed with talents very inferior to his. I early noticed in him a quiet but resolute ambition. Doubtless this greatly stimulated his natural love of learning; at the same time it appeared to me the great danger to which his character exposed him. At that time, however, I believe it was quite subordinate to his love of learning and his thirst for intellectual acquisition, and it did not much impress me. I have since been convinced that my judgment on this point was not unfounded." *

My son had now passed from the classes of the School to those of the College. His daily preparations for the work of the class-room were regular and thorough. He stood well as a prizeman, in one department or more, at the close of every session. When preparing for his examinations I had sometimes to rise from my own bed to urge him to retire to his. It was a point of some importance with me that he should not form the habit of studying late at night rather than early in the morning. He knew enough to satisfy him that conformity with my wishes in this particular would be advantageous to himself, and I may mention a

* Rev. J. H. Hutton.

circumstance connected with his effort in this respect, as tending to show the earnest spirit with which his studies were prosecuted, and the strength of purpose of which he was capable, when the occasion seemed to demand it. To ensure early rising, he placed an alarum on a bracket over the head of his bed, and near it a jug filled with water, and so connected the one with the other, that when the alarum ran down, the jug would overturn, and discharge its contents upon his pillow, if he did not at once rise to prevent it. The contrivance had its effect. He came by degrees, as a rule, to prefer working early to working late.

The following letter relates mainly to this stage in the career of the subject of this Memoir, and may be best introduced in this place. It is from the pen of W. C. Roscoe, Esq. a gentleman whose intelligence and culture were well known to a large circle of friends, and who was himself to be too soon numbered with the class of gifted men who are allowed to show to the world what they might be expected to do, and are then taken from among us.

"Derby, 15th Feb. 1858.

"MY DEAR SIR,

"I regret that I can furnish you with no materials for an estimate of Mr. Vaughan's character and labours at the time when they were fully matured and most important. During the time he was at college in London I was closely intimate with him; afterwards, however, distance of place, and difference of pursuits, made our opportunities of meeting very rare; but the warmth of friendship I entertained for him certainly never abated, and my profound esteem was gaining strength up to the time of his death, as I gathered from those few interviews I enjoyed, and from his occasional letters, how consistent and persevering his noble and self-devoted life was, and learned from a wider experience how rare and valuable such a life is.

"In his college studies he was chiefly remarkable for completeness and conscientious thoroughness in all he undertook. He had plenty of works of supererogation, but he *never* failed in what he sought to know. Whoever else failed, Vaughan might always be depended upon, and in any emergency the Professor would appeal to him with a confidence which I never remember to have seen disappointed. His mind took a far wider sweep than the ordinary college routine of subjects, and the range and accuracy of his knowledge in every branch of inquiry he took up were remarkable. His grave steadfastness of application and untiring industry were even then, I believe, based on a profound sense of religious responsibility; a feeling which grew deeper as his life advanced, and led to that entire and unsparing devotion of himself and all his faculties to the service of God, with which not only his duties as a minister of religion but all his other labours were discharged. Hence, nothing was unimportant to him, and all he did was done thoroughly and conscientiously.

"All this was accompanied with an unfailing cheerfulness, an ease and simplicity of manners, and a genuine cordiality that made him a most delightful companion. No man's society was more prized and more enjoyed in the brief intervals of leisure he allowed himself. His acquirements, his independent thought, and his lively imagination, made his conversation valuable; but to his enthusiasm on serious matters he added a liveliness and a quick sense of the ridiculous, and a genial mirthfulness which we then valued, probably, more than his higher qualities. His hearty and contagious laughter seems still to ring in my ears. He was devoted at that time to poetry, and the small volume of poems he published soon after leaving college remains to show how much fire of imagination he possessed; and when he found his vocation in another direction, this faculty still remained to give brilliancy and graphic force to his prose writings. I wish I could describe him better, and give a fuller idea of the manly self-sufficiency and breadth of character he possessed, the trustworthiness and purity of his heart, and the affectionateness of his disposition; but I cannot, and must be content with these few inadequate words of description. None of those who knew him in those early days but must have heard of his early death with the sincerest and profoundest regret; but he, if any man, worked while it is day, and accomplished the task which was committed to him. I believe no more faithful servant ever went to his rest.

"I am, my dear Sir, yours sincerely,

"WILLIAM C. ROSCOE.

"*The Rev. Dr. Vaughan.*"

Another of Alfred Vaughan's class-fellows, since conspicuous in public life, has informed me of an incident it may not be improper to mention. Mr. Key required the class to send in a Latin version of some English prose. The Professor complained of several of the papers as being far from satisfactory, but added that there was one paper of which he must speak in different terms. Mr. Vaughan's composition was so good that in reading it he could have thought he had been reading Cicero. My son was seen to blush deeply under such praise. But no jealousy was awakened. The class knew their Professor, and knew that no more had been said than might be justly said.

My son's connexion with University College extended to about six years. He matriculated early. In 1842 he took his B.A. degree, with honours in Classics, and in that department was the second man in the University of London for that year. He was still under twenty years of age.

But his attainments, and mental standing generally, at that time, were not to be measured by his academic standing. There are not a few men who reach a good position in University examinations, who never show themselves to be good at anything beside. They receive much, they produce nothing. There is scarcely anything for which their minds cannot find room, but there is no growth in them. So jostled are they by the crowding of other men's opinions as to lose the power of forming opinions of their own—so crammed with the contents of many books, that what might have been native in them is smothered as by an immense overgrowth. My son's mind was not of that order. His acquisitions became aliment to his inner life—means conducing to his personal culture. He always looked to the fruit of other men's labours in its relation to labours that were to be his own. Every gain had its value for him according to the measure in which it might prepare him for something he hoped himself to accomplish.

But in this stage of his progress there were what appeared to me defects in his mental tendencies. He passed his mathematical examinations satisfactorily, but he felt little interest in such studies. Nor was he disposed to think very highly of the uses of metaphysical speculation, or to attach great value to the study of psychology, or of formal logic. He seemed to have the impression that the best things taught in many of those departments were the things which everybody knew. Man in action was to him a far more significant and interesting subject than man taken to pieces. In brief, his æsthetic sympathies were strong, and his master passion at that time was the passion of the poet. He had made attempts in verse, but of the fragments which have survived it will be sufficient to adduce the following piece, written on the night that witnessed the departure of the year 1840 and the birth-time of 1841. It shows his religious feeling, as well as the complexion of his poetic taste, when not more than eighteen years of age.

ON THE NEW YEAR.

How hast thou stolen, ere we were aware,
Into our midst, oh year! How pale thy face!
How white thy feet and snow-besprinkled hair!
There is a timorous silence in thy face,
When climbing up to thy allotted place.
Thou settest in thy Hope-attended prime
The first adventurous foot on the old stage of Time.

Fain would I look to coming Sabbath-days,
Which God will measure to me one by one;
Will they be stars, shorn of their happy rays,
Encurtain'd by sin's mists,—or stand alone
Like evening clouds about a western sun,
All radiant with the beams of heavenly light,
When other days lie hid in long oblivious night?

And what shall be the memory of the hours
Spent in the house of God—oh! may they be

The heaven-planted, the undying flowers,
To make my wreath of immortality,
When these poor mortal eyes my Saviour see,
When this dim troublous dream of life is o'er,
And from my chainless soul drops sin for evermore.

Oh, Jesus! temper the rude hand of Death,
If it be ordered that this year I die,
Sweet Death will be, if soft are spread beneath
Thy loving arms, and the mild melody
Of thine own dying words is borne to me
By the faint notes of angel harps unseen,
Struck by departed friends, who first with Death have been."

The time had now come when it became necessary that my son should choose his path of occupation in life. His tastes disposed him to look in more than one direction. His sympathy with art, and the society familiar to him in London, prompted him to some study of the principles of taste generally, and to some practical effort as an artist. Some of his landscape sketches at that time gave promise of excellence. Judging from what he then produced, had he decided on being a painter, the wildest summits of the Alps, where vegetation struggles along the line of perpetual snows, and the dark and deep passes through which those ever-melting snows send their boisterous torrents, bearing earth, and rock, and tree before them, would have come out with beauty and sublimity from under his hand.

A friend who has survived him, in reviewing his life and writings, has touched very truthfully and happily on this phase of his sympathies:—

"Mr. Vaughan's love of the pencil, while it did not determine the profession in which his life was spent, being overruled by a higher motive, yielded to himself and friends in after life much profitable enjoyment. He plied his pencil with happy ease. The vignettes from his hand, illustrating his father's monograph of Wycliffe, are proofs of this. His intimate friends have had other proofs. We remember his thick note-book, stored with the records of his hurried travel through Italy; many of the sides of its pages are illuminated, like the ancient missals, with his pencillings by the way, and every fresh page is quaintly adorned at the top corner with a little square picture, such as amusingly introduces us to the fresh chapters of Thackeray's or Dickens's tales. These scenes are overrun with the humorous, as well as with the poetic spirit of the artist. He loved to draw a rare old ugly gargoyle, with its goblin face and blown out mouth, spouting down floods of water; or some of the laughable incidents by rail and steamboat, in streets and hotels, on Alpine mules and in Venetian gondolas, which kept a good-tempered traveller *en riant* continually. We would call attention to a well remembered morning we spent with him at Heidelberg, on his last visit to the Continent. It was only a few weeks before his death. He rode quietly up the winding path which leads to the gateway of the castle. Who that has stood beneath the shadow of that majestic palace, and wandered along its terraces, can disenchant his memory from the lingering spell? Happy morning! many even of the motley visitors, students, and native *bourgeois* who passed us, turned to look again at that pale face, whose outlines were so massive, but whose expression was so pure and gentle. The sunshine of the morning was pleasant to him, and awoke all the music of his soul. After sauntering quietly through the inner courts, and some of the dishevelled rooms of the gorgeous ruin, and hearing his descant upon its architecture and history—for to one so familiar with mediæval life, the statues and arabesque traceries of its splendid *façades*, the battlements without, the suites of building within, instantly revived the men who had built and inhabited the place, their manner of life, their ideas and deeds, of which all these things were but the fossil imprints—we sat down in a beautifully shaded and solitary part of the shrubberies, there to spend the day. Our seat commanded some of the most picturesque points of Elizabeth's garden and palace, and while his friends chatted with him, his sepia rapidly pictured the crumbling arches set with images and overhung with ivy. As was usual with him, both eye and hand found light and pleasant and useful work while his body rested; and these sketches are now the precious memorials of hours that were made happy by his joyous and sacred love. He often spoke of the great usefulness of the art of sketching to literary men, in not only deepening their sympathy with nature, but in giving exactness to their perceptions. The eye is insensibly taught to seize on the particular shapes and hues of every object as if it were about to transfer them to canvas, and so the mind retains a clear and vivid conception of it. They who are acquainted with his writings will feel that he spoke of his own experience in what he tells us concerning Goethe, who studied drawing for a time, but, like himself, afterwards left the pencil for the pen. 'In the woof of life,' he writes, 'the broken threads are gathered up, and woven again with care. Nothing is lost. Whether triumphant or abortive in detail, the curiosity, the ambition, the very imitation of youth, work towards the ripe production of wealthy age. Winckelmann contributed to "Wilhelm Meister," and the truth of many a description of nature may be traced to the crayon or the brush. The sketches of a poet are studies for poems. The eye acquires a new insight, and the memory a new retentiveness for form and colour, when the habit has been formed of long gazing on a landscape, while asking, how shall I preserve that gleam? how produce that blue? by what touches shall I indicate that particular foliage?'"

Among his poetical pieces, of an early date, is a series of verses under the title of the "Dying Painter." The descriptions in this piece set forth the passionate creations which never fail to have their place in the mind possessing a genius for art. The morning breaks on the lone dark room of the artist, and that day will be his last:—

"Consumption on his hollow cheek has thrown
  The hectic flush,—a signal unto Death
Quickly to come and enter on his own;
  And Life her wavering forces sheltereth
  Within his eyes, their mournful brows beneath,

Lighting them with a fire too falsely bright;
While Genius weeps beside her frail delight,
And strives in vain to guide his tremulous hand aright.

Full many a nightly hour was sleepless made,
Peopled with passionate imaginings,
For this last picture, where he had portrayed
Christ healing sickness. Suddenly the wings
Of a strange dimness shadow him, that brings
Flitting confused before his dizzy eyes,
An airy crowd of changing fantasies,
That rise and blend and fade, like fair cloud-pageantries.

And every form and every gorgeous scene
His pencil wrought, before him came, as ye
May round their dying father's bed have seen
Those who will soon be orphans. Stormy sea,—
And still deep waters, hidden lovingly,
From ominous star or sun, by hanging boughs,—
Wild rocks that tower'd, all scathed, with threatening brows,
Daring heaven's bolts once more their sulphurous wrath to rouse;—

Pictures of solemn, star-o'erwatchèd woods,—
Or crimson wings of brooding sunsets spread

O'er western islets set in perilous floods,
With scenes of human bliss or hate or dread;—
All that within his soul envisionèd,
His hand had painted, or had burn'd to paint,
Before his memory rise, then fading faint—
As things, though fair, with yet too much of earthly taint,—

Give place to this, his last, his noblest theme:
And now his eager fancy seems to see,
More bright than e'en in his most rapturous dream,
The awful pity, the meek majesty,
Of God's own Son,—O now, O now could he
Paint the conception that hath fired his brain!
But ah! that stricken hand is raised in vain—
The heart that felt that thrill will never beat again.

'Tis little now to him that all too soon
To win the fame so fondly sought he died,
And perish'd thirsting for too rare a boon;
How mean the world, the fame for which he sigh'd!
Look to that spirit gazing, eagle-eyed,
Upon his glory, whose afflicted mien
He strove when here to paint,—while every scene,
So witching fair on earth, doth only seem
As a marr'd image of some ill-remember'd dream."

There is room to fear that too much like this might have been the end of the writer himself had he chosen an artist's life. The uncertainties, and ups and downs so incident to that vocation, could not present an agreeable prospect to a mind so sensitive as his, and so little sanguine as to its own future. The effect, however, of this feeling in relation to art on his subsequent productions as a man of letters is very perceptible.

His admiration of effective public speaking was great; but the study of the law had no attraction for him: nor would his organization have been equal to the wear and tear inseparable from the life of a barrister much upon circuit; added to which, his religious character, as we have seen, had by this time become settled. While history in general was his favourite field of study, the section of that field in which he felt the greatest interest was the ecclesiastical. I did what I could to encourage him in that preference. It seemed reasonable to hope that he might thus be led by degrees to concern himself with those higher regions of thought which he had not hitherto been disposed to estimate at their real value. Church history not only gives us men in action, but in action to a large extent on grounds embracing great principles, and principles related to some of the most subtle forms of speculation. The man calling himself a theologian while affecting to despise metaphysics, simply proclaims his own folly.

The juncture at which my son had to come to his decision on this important matter was one of considerable mark and excitement. Great social changes had come, and were still in process. The hollow conventionalities of the reign of George IV.—that feeble collapse after the long death-struggle of the Napoleon war—had passed away. The Revolution in France under Charles X. had given its impetus to political feeling in Europe, especially in England. The Catholic Relief Bill had been carried, and concessions had been made to Protestant Nonconformists. The battle on the question of Parliamentary Reform, and of Municipal Reform, had been fought and won. The contest in relation to the great question of Free Trade was at its height. A strong tide had for some time set in on the side of Liberalism. Men's hopes and fears had become extravagant; everything was exaggerated. Liberals had learned to demand more than was reasonable. Conservatives were often in great fear where no fear was. One very conspicuous form assumed by these fears, amidst the action and reaction of the times, came up in the Tractarian controversy. The vain purpose of that movement was to prostrate Romanism by fighting it with its own weapons, and to sweep away Dissent as a nuisance under a religious name. Even the Evangelical clergy now added to their hereditary horror of Popery a scarcely less horror of Dissent. The Methodist body, too, shared in this feeling of alarm, and were much more with the past than with the present. In politics and religion, dispassionateness and candour were in those days very rare. Every indication of such feeling was denounced by extreme men as so much mean trimming or unfaithful compromise. In such seasons the sober-minded and the honest have to bide their time.

It was while the affairs of parties, political and religious, were in this posture that my son felt constrained to look to the work of the Christian ministry.

This disposition came mainly from his religious feeling. But in his case, as in many more, there were subsidiary considerations which had their weight. How many men become clergymen to a large extent from their utter distaste for the coarse collision and vulgar brawl with which they would often be mixed up in other pursuits? What they covet in the Christian ministry, is its comparative quiet, and the sense of being useful without taking much part in the worldly contentions ever going on about them. It is well, no doubt, that among the ministers of religion there should be men of courage, capacity, and knowledge of affairs, capable of sustaining the interests especially entrusted to them in the presence of the powers that be, whatever they may be. But the men of this sort needed are the exception, not the rule. The pastoral life in its ordinary routine makes only a moderate demand on such qualities. My son was not wanting in courage. He could, I believe, have gone to the block or the stake for a great principle. But he was not formed, either in body or mind, for taking a prominent place in the rough encounters of public life. He greatly admired the qualities which fitted some men for being quite in their element in the midst of such scenes. He could enter into the spirit of the struggle, could delineate its passions, and describe its action, with great truth and force. But he felt that his own vocation did not lie in taking part with such actors. At the same time, what some men would have construed in him as timidity, or a love of ease, was really something different, and something much better. It was a love of quiet for the sake of thought, and for the sake of the kind of usefulness to be realized by thought. He knew that there was nothing necessarily discordant between ministerial duty and his literary tastes. He always regarded his capabilities and tastes as a Divine bestowment, and never ceased to feel himself responsible for the best possible application of them. He knew that the Christian priesthood should be, at least in the case of a portion of its members, eminently a priesthood of letters, and that in giving himself to the work of the preacher and the pastor, it might behove him to endeavour to do service to religion in many ways beyond those limits. It is, I conceive, deeply to be regretted that notions should prevail concerning religious office, which seem to say that in such cases the man should be merged in the minister, the patriot in the priest. In all ages the Church has needed the services of men of far higher type than that, and the Head of the Church has not failed to send them into his vineyard, and has given them their work to do.

The following passages from my son's diary will show the feeling of self-consecration with which he gave himself to his work as a minister of Christ at this juncture :—

"*April 3rd*, 1843.—My object must be to look on myself as *called* by my Redeemer to set myself apart for his ministry, looking up to Him my only hope; to pray that I may do his will concerning me. How can I be disobedient to the will of such a Master? One day I shall be with Him alone, I shall be casting myself on his righteousness as all my help; let me then now unite my heart to fear his name by the help of the promised Spirit. I should not have been satisfied that I was doing right if I had been anything but what I am about to become. And is not that a call? Could I but look up to Him with constancy as the Redeemer who is indeed my salvation, and to whom I ought to devote every capability—what success will be produced by the concentration—what good with the success—what joy with the good! The fruits of this decision would probably surpass all I have dared to hope. O God! grant it me—grant it me!

"*Sunday, July 17th*, 1843.—I earnestly desire to devote every capability in the utmost to Christ—to spend my life in the immediate service of such a Master, and, as far as my poor ability goes, to be made useful to the cause of his truth in my day and generation. I consider NO labour too great to endure for the realization of success as a preacher of the gospel. In that occupation alone do I expect happiness, because then alone can I be most entirely devoted in my gratitude to the Redeemer. It is my fervent hope that my weakness may be made strength in so great a cause. To be presented faultless, unblameable! And by what means? At what cost?

"What is the beautiful or the great of earth compared with this? Here is a subject, at the very least, worthy all the puny powers of any child of man. *Well* may angels desire to look therein. This is the thing, whatever we remember, which we mortals are constantly forgetting—this is the thing which I wish constantly to proclaim, and to ring it in men's ear till I die. This is the thing of which I hope ever to have such a growing conviction myself, that no prosperity, or adversity, or chance, or change of this life, may be able to shake my humble trust in Him in whom I have trusted, or obscure my increasing knowledge of Him in whom I have believed.

"*Sunday, July 24th.*—Sheppard recommends, when we would indulge devotion, and are distressed by an unsurmountable preoccupation of the mind, that we endeavour to make our devotion partake of the nature of that preoccupation rather than seek to run directly counter—to take advantage of that in tacking which would effectually bar all progress if our souls were squared against it. Thus, in my own instance, Poetry, which so much absorbs my thought, as indeed all intellectual engagements must in their nature do, may be made use of as a means of elevating my thoughts to Him who made the poet, and the nature which the poet pictures, and who must be so far more beautiful than the genius of the one or the realities of the other; or, again, it may be poetry consecrated to his service, and endeavouring to invest with all the interest that imagination, harmony, and fancy can throw about the subjects of a sacred nature.

"*October 17th*, 1843.—I feel the necessity of self-confidence. I am determined to possess it. How many inferior minds have succeeded because they could push on with undaunted assurance. Relying on Christ, I *will* become an efficient preacher of his gospel. I *will* succeed, nothing shall deter me. I will shrink from no sanguine vision, and accompany my high hopes with a concentrated and tireless effort. I am confident that it is in my power, and it is my duty, and shall be my happiness to struggle with a determination not to be weakened, with a spirit not to be repressed."

It was in this spirit that my son became a student in the Lancashire Independent College, in 1843, the year in which the opening of that College was inaugurated, and in which I became its President. The full course of study extended to five, sometimes to six years. But as my son had graduated in arts, his entrance, according to the rule in such cases, was only for the theological course, which was restricted to three years. During those years, his previous acquisitions made it easy for him to keep pace with the work of the class-room. But the history of his mind during this interval was far from being included in such exercises.

His religious feeling was deep and strong, much more so, as now appears from his diaries, than the persons about him at the time supposed. In some seasons it was of a happy description, full of hope, and of Christian aspiration. In others his upbraidings of himself were severe, and must have been attended by much pain. And there were intervals, it appears, in which his hope as a Christian seemed to be all but extinct. The many hours in the day, and sometimes in the night, which he gave to study of one kind or another, and the earnestness with which he endeavoured to make himself master of everything he took up, must have made a perilous demand on one whose physical strength was so limited. But his chief danger in this respect did not come from that source. More exhausting than the labour of the study must have been the action of that constant forecasting, of that extreme sensitiveness, and that ever-fluctuating hope and fear which seem to have been almost inseparable from his nature. His resolution at times mounts to the heroic. He can brave anything—endure anything. But the influences about him change, his spirit droops, and the sense of drooping becomes only the more painful from the contrast to the antecedent elevation. Not that these fluctuations were such as to disturb the general current of his tastes and purposes. These continue fixed in the main through it all, but fixed as a standard remains fixed in a battle-field, by much hard fighting to sustain it. He sometimes doubts how far he is to be successful as a Christian minister, or as a Christian poet, but his constant feeling is, that if he is to excel in anything it must be in these things. Sometimes the relative place of these two objects is a little changed in his anticipations and plans, but they always go together. A few passages from his diaries will suffice to make the reader acquainted with the complexion of his religious history from 1843 to 1846:—

"*Nov. 15th*, 1843.—The years are gliding away from me. This one will soon be gone. I shall soon be twenty-one. What have some men done before that age? What shall I have done? When all the years of my life shall have passed, and I come to review them on my death-bed—what is it I ought to see? What is it I should love to see? A life during which I have written poetry that has thrilled men's hearts with a love of all that is beautiful and good and godlike,—a life during which I have humbly and devotedly served Christ, and converted many souls.

"*Nov. 27th*, 1843 (Sunday).—Yesterday's well-spent remembrance puts me in good state for to-day's sipping at Heaven's streams. I seem now to have a definite object, viz.—to spend my days showing my grateful love to Christ by working with all my energies for Him, who is my one hope, my one friend. How far, then, ought I to be above all meanness of spirit, all narrowness of prejudice, all grovelling of affection? My life should be spent for Him who is my joy. I should lie as in His bosom, and may the murmurs of gratitude that may escape my weak lips there make an echo in many a devout soul. That is the crown of glory for which I strive—the laurel of Christian poetry, with the sweet-toned voice amidst the day of judgment, saying, 'Well done, good and faithful servant.' Oh, what unutterable joy! How my mind falls back lost in the thought of it; how trivial time, how weak sin, how unlovely allurement, compared with this! Oh for that 'perfect witness of all-judging love.'

"*Dec.* 18*th.*—Afternoon—read a sermon of Barrow's on 'Ascended into heaven and sitteth at the right hand of God,' &c. Some good things—a scholarlike performance, and as well-adapted for reading as ill-adapted for preaching. Evening—my father at home; gave us a beautiful exposition of the twenty-third Psalm. Oh to realize something of the *grandeur* of God's truth—to be more at home in it—to find my element and delight in the study of it and its proclamation. Christ, the heir (says Barrow), has entered on the inheritance—we, his retinue, are to follow.

"*July*, 1844.—I cannot now read too much of my Bible and of good sermons. Would to God I could more practise what I preach and teach. Intellectually I may suffice—oh for more of the piety of many I have despised. Beware of conceit! God and myself only know how much I have to sink me in the dust before the meanest. But the die is cast. Nothing now shall turn me back. My Saviour not casting me out—what shall stay me? God preserve me from resting satisfied with myself a moment on this side the grave.

"*July*, 1846.—Thanks to God for more lively faith, a more earnest spirit of prayer, a deeper joy in religion, more self-renunciation. . . . How have I been delighted, elevated, calmed! A thousand impure thoughts chased away, affection turned to a true, noble, pure channel, joy from the highest source above, from the best on earth, poured in on me from every side. In preaching most of joy and success, shown by the approval and wishes of those I have addressed. Guilty as I was, God has interposed—snatched me from the utmost peril of vileness and thanklessness, given me love to Him and love to others. Oh what shall I render to the Lord. Let me be thine; teach me still more; shine on me still more brightly. Let me never again go so far from Thee as I have gone, but keep me with thine embrace now and ever."

This last extract presents the writer to us in one of his

happiest seasons; but, as his language implies, it was not always thus with him. There was a time for the cloud as well as for the sunshine, as the following passage, written a little *before*, will show :—

"*June*, 1844.—Matters cannot go on as they have done. I am now going to see whether there be any truth in the Bible or not; whether what we preach of a Saviour who intercedes and helps men against sin be a cunningly devised fable or not. If there be any help or love in Jesus I must have it, for I have entreated it, and none ever could need it more. I have all that can move his compassion in my vile helplessness, and if I am not helped now there can be no Saviour. Better annihilation, or never to have heard of Him, than to find that there is no help against the power of sin. Hear me now in this, oh! Supreme Friend, or it will be my lot to curse the hour of my birth. Oh, hearer and answerer of prayer, how can I teach sinners thy ways if thou wilt not teach me thyself. I dare not doubt thy compassion, oh, dying Christ! If I had not known *Thee*, I had not known sin. Thy goodness has made me fearfully guilty, Oh carry on that goodness, or I perish evermore. One word could do it. Holder of the keys of life and death, hast Thou not that word in the heart that feels for the whole universe? Oh, Christ, thou knowest what hell is—wilt thou not hear me pleading against being driven hither? Help my unbelief, by showing thou canst hear and save from sin. Amen."

These diaries contain other entries, which, as I have intimated, give expression to the feeling of self-distrust and depression on the part of the writer; but nothing betraying grief so deep, dark, and terrible as the above. Few who knew him suspected that the soul, regarded as pure and devout so much beyond the ordinary measure, had known what it was to be led through such depths. But it is not difficult now to see that such experiences were to have their use in his after life. They were part of the discipline which made him ultimately what he was.

It will be seen from the preceding extracts that nothing gave him greater pleasure than to know that his attempts to preach the Gospel effectually had been successful. But even in this connexion he often felt discouraged. His youthful presence, his agreeable voice, his singularly natural elocution, the wisdom beyond his years which seemed to breathe through many of his utterances, and the richness of the illustrations often supplied by his imagination and fancy, sufficed to render his pulpit services generally nteresting, in not a few cases deeply so. Nothing gratified him more than to know that the common people heard him gladly. It was then that he ventured to think that his preaching must have borne some resemblance to that of his Divine Master. Preaching on one occasion in a village chapel, a pious old woman, at whose house he stayed, said to him, 'Ye 'are a vera nice mahn in t' pulpit, and I should loike to 'hear ye reglar;' and added, says the preacher, 'what 'was to me best of all, that she understood every word.' On another occasion, when fearful that his sermon might not be readily intelligible to the less instructed among his hearers, he felt himself greatly encouraged, he writes, in seeing a grey-headed mechanic before him, in very humble garb, so attentive as to seem to be drinking in every word. The following extract will go far to explain the secret of such interest:—'Last night finished a 'sermon begun on Thursday evening. I think the best 'I have yet written. In more than one passage I was 'myself moved to tears in reading it this morning. God 'make it useful.' Sermons so prepared cannot be sermons without power. Yes, and the young preacher could find his philosophical, as well as his Christian reasons, for being interested in the piety even of minds thus humble.

"*Dec. 23rd*, 1844.—If a man has an enthusiasm for poetry he will dig up the precious gems though buried in the soil of an obsolete style, or lying among the mysteries of some foreign or dead language. He will hold communion, and feel himself one in the matter of poetic fancy, with men who in every other respect were different beings from himself, men who were moulded in bygone customs, and whose whole cast of mind took its tone from the youth of the world which we call remote antiquity. But if this be done for the sake of poetry, surely we should be prepared to give an echo in our heart to true religion, to acknowledge its happy spark though shrouded in the mist and errors of some past age, or associated with a rude lowliness."—*Diary.*

It must be confessed, however, that at intervals it was not on sermons, nor on theological papers, that my son bestowed the most elaborate attention. His passion for poetry never ceased to exert great influence over him. Before leaving London he had written poetry, and contributed fragments to several periodicals. In 1844, while only in his twenty-first year, he prepared a small volume of poetry for publication. It was entitled *The*

Witch of Endor, and other Poems. He was admonished, that should he venture to print, he would probably live to see that it would have been better to have exercised a little more patience. He admitted this probability, but thought there were other considerations that outweighed it. He had the impression that if he was to do anything eventually in authorship, it became him to face criticism early, and to expect proficiency only from practice.

The fault of the poetry in this volume is an overcrowding of metaphor, in a want of clearness and simplicity. The metaphors are often highly poetical, and indicate an unusual richness of fancy and imagination. But their tendency is sometimes to overlay thought rather than to express it. No one could be more sensible to this imperfection than the writer himself in after years. The volume, however, contains passages which could only have been written by a mind of high poetical capability. As the publication is now out of print it may be well to quote an extract or two, in confirmation of this statement. The following is the opening of the principal poem :—

SAUL, DOEG, AND NAHOR.

The heights of Endor by moonlight. Saul and his attendants stand on the edge of a deep ravine.

DOEG.

My royal master, hard by here she dwells,
Of whom the needy mountaineers informed us,
With many fears and tremblings at her vengeance,
That yielded to our gold. Look down, my lord,—
There, in the misty depths of this vast chasm
Over whose edge we lean, a threading stream
Winds dimly, and to the imprisoned darkness
Held there by these twin, almost meeting rocks,
Gives with its silver footsteps mournful light.
That rivulet is born, as we were told,
Out of the heart of a weird cavern, arched
Under the base of the broad cliff before us,
And in that cave she holds her incantations,
And by it is her hut beneath a crag-cleft,
The mountain way which down this rock-side leads
They showed us,—shall we now descend and learn
If in her den she holds? When she was there,
And when away, they knew not, only that
Of late she hath been thought to keep herself
More closely hidden, since the camp came hither.

SAUL.

Yes—down at once; but steal a careful path,
Within the shadows treading without word,
Lest ye should startle your mistrustful prey
Into some hiding-place that baffles quest;
Then hither,—and await me if not here.

NAHOR.

There's a wild fearfulness in these gaunt rocks,
And their grim-sleeping shadows crouched beneath them.
There's not a hollow or height that might not make
A spirit's fitting haunt. May it please thee
That I remain to be thy sentinel,
And hold my faithful watch 'gainst any ill
Lurking in wait for thine anointed person?

SAUL.

Peace, thou presuming prater!—What! dost think
Because some windy darkness lowers above us,
And trouble late hath come with stranger face
To pass a brief hour, that we shake—we bend,
And every puny insect of the field
Must run to prop us up? We need not thee,
Nor any of thy kind,—away, and know
Saul only shows more firm and wintry stern
For all the leaves ill chance may blow from him.

[*Exeunt* DOEG *and* NAHOR.

SAUL.

O, fool, fool, fool!—one time 'twas not my wont
To be so idle-passionate: I angered men
With deeds, not words.
How mournfully this breeze
Steals up the heights, and brings me from the vale
The bark of watch-dogs in the distant camp,
Waking no hope, foretaste of victory,—
Only reminding me of my despair!
Each soldier there may slumber in deep rest,
As oft he hath on battle-eves gone by;
But I—a Power, an inmost Influence
That tarried with me, hath pursued its flight,
And borne away the mantle of soft sleep.

Saul presently rejoins Doeg and Nahor, and inquires if they have found the Witch. Nahor replies:—

NAHOR.

My lord, unseen have we been watching her,
Within her naked miserable hut,
Stooped down, and holding out her withered hands
O'er a few embers, as she hummed the while
Some low monotonous ditty. When the flame
Would ever and anon leap, flashing on her,
She looked so haggard, gaunt, and hunger-pinched,
Doubtless there's nought but she would dare for gold.

The scene that follows is thus described :—

The hut of the Witch, who is discovered within.

Enter SAUL, DOEG, *and* NAHOR.

THE WITCH, *who sees them and rises.*

The badge of Saul! Ah, ye have found me, have ye?
Three murder-hunting hounds with bloody clutches
Watched to bring down the relict of a remnant
In this poor lair! Did ye not find enough
When last ye stamped your red steps on these mountains?
May dæmon-driven blasts ride out and meet you,
And blow their dust of curses in your eyes,
Up to your joy remorse climb after you,
A dread death track you out as ye have me.
May every—

SAUL.

Stay—indeed thou wrong'st us: hear me;
I am a man this earth of late hath shaken
With such rough shocks of quick-succeeding griefs,
I fain would rise into the solemn air
Of the dim future, and I pray thee help me.
The stars that guide most men are dark to me,
And lost in night I drive tempestuously
Up towards the doubtful lights of thine enchantments.
Call up for me—

WITCH.

Yes, yes, thou fain wouldst catch
My misery with a tale of misery,
As men make fish the bait for simple fishes.
I fear not to acknowledge what I am—
Did I not so just now? Ye need not wait
To see me do some witchery, and then take me.
My life I love not, take it, ye are welcome,—
And be it to you the burden it hath been
Of late to me. I pray you take all here,—
The poor utensils of this poorer hut,
Or search for hidden treasure till ye're weary.

SAUL.

'Twas no thieves' errand brought us here, unless
To rob thee of this poverty be a theft,
And fill thy widest expectation up
With overflowing gold, if thou wilt serve me.

WITCH.

Doubtless thy wealth has been to thee a curse,
That thou'rt so hot to thrust it upon me.

SAUL.

O woman, woman! is a drop of pity
Left in thy hard, affliction-scorchèd heart?
With tears I pray thee—let my tears augment it?

A proud wave, broken, clasps these rocky feet.—
Hast thou been outlawed, hunted down, forsaken?
Oh! I have been unhoused from every hope,
Been cursed, and my swift, happy hours have been
Chased out of time by swifter-wing'd despairs,
The spirits thou canst rule have been my torment,
Pursued where thy pursuers could not come,
Crowded all ghastly on my solitude.
Misery with misery should have sympathy.
Nay, spurn me not—wealth, honour, followers,
The things men trust in, all do I let go
And cling to thy compassionate dark power—
My last, last hope. Hast thou e'er struggling prayed
In vain for help in thine extremity?
Wound not with that keen steel thyself hast felt;
If 'tis a crime to grant my piteous prayer
I am as deep in guilt for making it.
These men are faithful, this night's work, sealed up,
For my sake must lie hushed as well as thine.

WITCH.

Have I known suffering? Has my need been scorned?
Ay—night and day they drove us up and down,
Butchered us one by one; in every brake,
Wild, height, and cave spread nets of death for us.
I've made my bed in caverns, holes, and pits,
In thorns, and mire, and clefts too rough for beasts,

To 'scape the spring-tide flood of massacre.
Breathless and bloody past my hiding-place
I saw Saul's soldiers hurry many a time.
They dashed my little ones against the rocks—
E'en as they smiled upon their savage faces.
They chased my hoary father to the death—
They came upon my husband as he fled—
Hard by these rocks it was, and stoned him there.
Oh! when will vengeance smooth the memory
Of how that night I did creep forth, and found
The heapèd monument of stones that hid
The bruised and bleeding mass; and as I pulled,
With careful hand, the jaggèd flints away,
His hairs with hardened gore were stuck to them!
How cursed I Saul as underneath that moon,
So oft the witness of my vain enchantments,
Those ragged remnants of his flesh I buried!
Again I curse him, in the coming fight
May his red hand hang withered by his side!
Stay—hear me, I was lonely, none to pity,
And then had perished but for these poor hinds,
Who, part from fear and part that oftentimes
I cured their ailments with some simple medicine,
Covered my need with many kindnesses.

The witch is at length prevailed upon to invoke her spirits, and to call for the appearance of Samuel, and the answer of the invisible ones may be taken as a sample of the lyric power of the poet:—

Chill thy charm and weak thy words,
  Back thy powerless spells we fling,
Angel looks and cherub swords
  Guard the soul thou bidst us bring.
Bid us bring thee mortals lost
  From the fire-beds where we threw them,
Shrieking from our grasp out-tossed:—
  Where above them weltering
Loud flame-rivers leap and roar,
And like garments spread them o'er,
And drink their weepings evermore,
  And thy daring eyes shall view them
If him alone thou'dst look upon,
We are gone——

Other Spirits.

    To the cedar-shadows gone
Under the howlings of Lebanon,
To spin the web that shall be spun
By which human souls are won,
    Many a one
    May be foredone
Ere the morning bring the sun—

Other Voices.

To the Sea dark, heavy, and dead,
Where the fire-flooded cities lie,
Where the birds that o'er it fly
And all things living die,
We are fled—fled,
To sit under tempests there,
And think, as they blackly roar,
We sweetly hear once more,
As it rose on their day of doom,
The cry of their wild despair
Peal through the gloom.—

Other Spirits sing in fainter tones.

We are fled—fled,
We mock at the charge thou hast given ;
It is weak as the summer when dead
To stay the storms of heaven,—
On which will we ride to-night,
Like the leaves that are on them shed,
Will we ride to-night——

A distant Voice.

To-night !

Much of promise as there was in such poetry, it appeared to me desirable that my son should be induced to take up some topic in prose with the same earnest spirit. Among my books was a copy of Delarue's edition of the works of Origen; and by my advice Alfred began the study of those stately folios, with the intention of writing a review article on the life and works of that great man. His reading for this purpose was patient and thorough, and the article, though the production throughout of a young man not yet twenty-two years of age, was founded, I have reason to believe, on a better knowledge of the opinions of that Father than was possessed at that time by any other man in England. This was my son's first contribution to the *British Quarterly Review*. The following letter presents a criticism on this paper from the pen of Sir James Stephen, written a few weeks after its publication :—

"Downing-street, Nov. 5th, 1845.

"MY DEAR FRIEND,

I must send you one further line to say that, since I last wrote to you, I have read your son's paper on Origen, which confirmed one of my clearest opinions —namely, that the generation of men who are just coming into active life have an immense advantage over the generation which took that step thirty years ago. At that time there was no youth of my own acquaintance, I believe there was none living, who could have produced (there was certainly none who did produce) a composition so full of sound learning, so highly wrought up, without any tawdry ornament, and so continually progressing (the Yankees should be thanked instead of ridiculed for the word) from one firm and weighty meaning to another. If I had been told that the writer of it was a grandfather, I should have wondered only that the old gentleman had retained so much spirit, and been able to combine it with a maturity of judgment so well becoming his years. The only objection I can make to the style is that occasionally the landmarks between prose and poetry are thrown down, although the image of the violet and the weeping willow is so very pretty, that it was not in poor weak human nature to resist the temptation. The whole composition has also a breadth and Catholic spirit about it in which I greatly delight. Yet I cannot think that the subject was very well chosen for a review. The mere biography afforded few materials; and all the description of Alexandria, splendid as it is, has too plainly the mark of being pressed into the service to atone for that inherent defect. The doctrine, on the other hand, is unavoidably, but yet unpleasantly, compressed into a space too narrow for its development. Has your son a copy of what I take to be the dullest book ever written on a most attractive theme—I mean Cave's *Lives of the Fathers of the Fourth Century?* If not, I will gladly make him a present of that *caput mortuum*, on condition that he will galvanize it. Each of the heroes of the very learned and drowsy Rector of Isleworth would pass beautifully into a portrait; and the whole, when collected together, might make as charming a book as there is in our language.

"Ever yours,

"JAMES STEPHEN.

"Rev. Dr. Vaughan."

About the same time I received a letter in relation to this article from Mr. Serjeant, afterwards Judge Talfourd, from which the following extract is taken. Both these gentlemen knew my son from his early boyhood:—

"It was wise in you to suggest and direct his attention to such a subject, even if it had been less ably treated. It is nobly done. I scarcely ever remember to have read an essay by any young man so rich in promise for the future. If there is some exuberance of ornament in the setting forth of his brilliant theories, it is only akin to the irregular greatness and the Asiatic splendour of the mind which conceived them; and at the same time, no industry has been spared to present these things in their historical truthfulness. There is also a candour of spirit highly commendable in his judgment of those errors which were mixed up with so much greatness."

Encouraged as he was by such appreciation of his capacity as a prose writer, Alfred still retained much of his old love of poetry. Among the fragments produced by him while in Lancashire was a dramatic piece intitled "Edwin and Elgiva," which appeared in the *London University Magazine* in 1846; and the "Masque of Antony" and the "Disenchantment," which are printed for the first time in his "Remains," were then written.

My son was a great admirer of "Comus," and the "Masque of Antony" is such a piece as a classic poet might be supposed to have written on the shores of the Mediterranean two thousand years ago. It embodies the popular belief of those times. No modern reader must be expected to be interested in the mythological fictions of this poem; but the poetry may not be the less real because lavished on a theme which, though once a religious creed, is such no longer. The writer, at the time, was fresh from his classical studies, and, I should perhaps add, was a great admirer of the poetry of Shelley. Nemesis is about to subject Antony, Cleopatra, and Alexandria to their doom, and several divinities deprecate the coming vengeance. The following is the opening speech of Nemesis, who appears above the city of Alexandria.

"*Time, Midnight.*

From your ever-falling fountains,
  Where the moonbeams cannot rest;
From your emerald thrones, the mountains,
  Where the storm in clouds is drest;
From your continents and islands,
  By the fickle waves carest;
From your winter-haunted highlands,
  From the cloud-home of the blest;
Come ye gods of earth and water,
  Come ye gods of wood and hill,
For the weeping and the dying
  Shall be many on the morrow,
In the city that is lying
  In the slumber of its sorrow."

The river-god Cydnus pleads as follows in favour of the Egyptian queen:—

Let her beauty on my wave
Be a token that shall save,

And the pleading of my river
Make thee pity and forgive her,
For beneath her and above her
Sky and water join to love her.
I was at a noon-day sport
With the naiads of my court,
As they wove me crowns of reeds
Interstrung with pearly beads,
When on a sudden I was ware
Of a bark that passed above,
And of music in the air,
Whereunto the ship did move,
And of beauty sitting there
That did make the music love.
  Up I looked, and saw the lines
Of the silver oars each side,
While the sail that hung between
From me hid the lovely queen
As a cloud doth intervene,
Coming underneath the moon:
But with many a ray full soon
On each side she overshines,
And, like oars, I've seen the beams
Send their sidelong silver gleams
Slanting through the airy tide."

* * * *

These extracts will sufficiently indicate the character and execution of the poem.

When my son had completed his course of three years in the theological classes of the Lancashire Independent College, it appeared to me desirable that he should pass a year in some German university, before committing himself to the distractions and responsibilities of a pastorate. Some good men may be disposed to question the soundness of my judgment in this particular. That a youth of not more than three-and-twenty should be committed to the study of German theology in the heart of a German university, and not be deeply injured by the process, may be, in the view of such persons, to the last degree improbable. But the wisdom or the folly of such a step must depend very much on the character of the mind to be exposed to such contact. My son had already become familiar, to a considerable extent, with German theology. Very little was left to come up from German professors that could take him by surprise. In so far as I then knew his mind, his thoughtful piety, his fixed reverence for the authority of the sacred Scriptures, and that caution and ripeness of judgment which began thus early to characterize him, seemed, when taken together, quite enough to show that, in his case, such a course might be advisedly taken.*

It was clear to me that England was destined to be agitated by nearly all the theological questions which had been so much discussed in Germany. It seemed to me no less certain that the men best qualified to refute the errors of German theologians

* The following devout thoughts were addressed to a friend at this juncture, concerning the death of a youth in a family much esteemed by the writer: 'Believe me how I feel for you and for them. I have entered into the shadow along with you. I stand beside the coffin of one I never saw, yet love. I am in the quiet darkened house of mourning. I hear only the ticking of the clock —marking that which is no more now to the dead one. It is the parting point of the two portions of sundered mortality—the pathway divides—the soul travels its path, the body also—the ways meet again at God's gate. For the taken, God be praised; for the left, God be pitiful. There is one less of those loved to fear for—one less to pray trembling for. There is a world of truth in those three words—'one more safe!' The body safe past pain—the soul safe past sorrow. In a glory he shines past conceiving—in a fruition past prayer. But of what others we love can we say they are safe? In utmost grief it is yet a blessing that there is one more we can say that of. God smile the bereaved hearts into peace! Where life's green has been scathed may Heaven's dew fall!'

must be, for the most part, the men who have taken most pains to make themselves familiar both with the errors and the truths to be found in writers of that class. Such is the discrepancy natural to all false theories, and such the iconoclastic spirit of our German neighbours, that the source of the poison has naturally become the best source for the antidote. My hope was, that as the result of his German studies, my son would prove capable of rendering me efficient aid in my endeavours to sustain the interests of revealed truth through the press.

CHAPTER II.

STUDIES IN HALLE.

1846—1847.

THE route taken for Halle was through Hamburgh and Bremen, as two of my daughters were to be left by their brother in the latter city. As this was the first time Alfred had seen a continental town, he was busy in his observation of the novelties which came before him. He had read much concerning the manners of countries different from his own, but he had not seen the contrasts which were to become familiar to him.

"*Sept.* 14. The Hamburgh people," he writes, "are inconceivably indolent, and fond of amusement. It takes three or four of them to do the work of one Englishman. The environs of the town are very pleasant, laid out with long avenues of trees, where there are crowds of people, especially on the Sabbath. There are also a great number of theatres and dancing-rooms, all open on the Sunday, and well attended. It is remarkable how much more time the people spend in the open air here than in England, smoking, coffee-drinking, needlework, and even reading by lamp-light outside the house. I understand the English residents here have fallen but too much into the German practice as regards the Sabbath. The servants have all the character of arrant pilferers.

"I think I may, with reason, expect great benefit from these travels, inasmuch as they are likely to give me that practical readiness and managing faculty of which a life among books, and devoid of action, has left me almost wholly destitute.

"S——, the young Englishman now preaching here, gave me an appalling account of the ill effects produced on himself by a year's cessation from preaching, while he was attending lectures at Glasgow. It cannot be helped. All I can do is to endeavour that it shall not be so with me."

Writing to the same friend, and about the same time, he says:—

"I have been thinking somewhat concerning the objects which, during my stay in Halle, I must keep mainly in view—the manner and the mode of the self-improvement I contemplate. If I can accomplish all I intend, it will be well. If it be possible (and why should it not) to attain a greater relish for processes of reasoning and the arguments of abstract speculation (which it is a great deficiency in my mind not to enjoy), without at the same time losing a certain enthusiasm and warmth of fancy which gives me much delight, I shall return to England with a mind of greater robustness and hardihood, and be more armed at every point for mutual effort. My intellect has gone out too much in one direction,—namely, that most easy to me—just whither imagination and phantasy may lead. The difficulty I perceive with regard to many other species of application is the very reason why I should more sedulously attempt them. Both as an author and as a preacher, it is what I require. Of course, every man must do mainly what he does *best;* but at the same time what he does best will be better done for doing other things well too. The faculties go very much together, and the cultivation of one will often direct the exercise of another. I am conscious of a sort of inverse in my intellectual character,—that which ought to be first is with me second, and the second first. A great error this, because the brilliance of fancy is quite useless without a vigorous reason and well-disciplined judgment. There is a danger of my being more anxious to interest than to instruct—to collect a multitude of materials for adorning the edifice, and quite to forget that the carts have not yet come up with the stone which must make the strength and be the substratum of the whole. The secret of the deficiency I am willing to believe is rather indolence than incapacity. To correct myself in these respects will be a foremost aim with me while abroad, seeing that fixed stars are more serviceable than comets."

In his diary of the same date, he writes:—

"The object on which I am resolved is, first, earnest discriminating thought, especially exercised concerning reasoning and metaphysical subjects. Neither let this, I may supplementarily observe, chill the heart. Let me, by God's help, nourish that sensitive plant to a greater breadth of unfolding. Let me not expect, as a thing of course, to have less religion under the disadvantages there; but resolve with help to have more—a feeling more ardent, and more enlightened views concerning God's truth in general."

Such was the feeling and intention with which my son became a student in the University of Halle, in the autumn of 1846. He soon found that if Glasgow, so rich in pulpit light and power, had been so unfavourable to the piety of the mere student, in the case of Mr. S——, the atmosphere of Halle was such as to make watchfulness against evil in that form specially important.

"*Oct.* 11. It is Sunday. We went out into the Sabbath worship of nature, after being in the house which is devoted to the Sabbath worship offered by man. The interior of the place was a cold white—some rude white panels in some places, and whitewash in others—with wretched images of Virgin and saints, decked out in tawdry coloured dresses and gold crowns; half-obliterated pictures, which beneath their indistinctness had no grace; an organ which, for the absurd finery of its ornaments, would have been out of taste in a theatre; and a crucifix before which the minister knelt—these things composed the apparatus of the worship. To this must be added that in this place, capable of seating about six or seven hundred persons, there were scarcely a hundred, and those seated in a scattered way, so as rather to add to the frigidity of the general scene than to diminish it. And this was Protestantism! The Lutheran Church in Germany. A short liturgy, consisting of a few prayers, the Creed, and our Lord's Prayer, together with psalmody, preceded the sermon. One of the hymns we sung was an eminently beautiful composition, rich in devotional sentiment. After the close of the Liturgy the long tapers on the altar were extinguished, and at the conclusion of another hymn the preacher commenced his discourse. It was founded on the words, 'What think ye of Christ? Whose son is He?' and he insisted with fervour, even with tears, on the preciousness of our belief in Him as divine. In all the other places to which we have been, the attendance has been equally wretched—a mere handful of people in the largest places. How I thought of England! We see here the effects of Rationalism."

Some weeks later he writes:—

"*Sunday morning.*—Have just returned from all but an empty church, without any edification. When shall I enjoy an English service again? If I am spared to return, I will preach more of what is called the Gospel than I did before. The talk about adapting religion to the times, which is prevalent here even among the religious, appears to me a miserable mistake. It never needed adapting so much as when the Apostles preached it. But they made no such effort."

It should be added, that an exception to this dreary state of things was found in the church where Professor Tholuck preached. His congregation was always large, and the service in his hands was eminently edifying and devout. Of the English and German mode of life in general, Alfred remarks, that they are in two extremes.

"The Englishman is a little too practical, the German too speculative and recluse. A learned man who, with all his learning, would starve in England, in Germany is honoured. On the other hand, of our popular religious life they know little here. Upon our theology and ecclesiastical literature generally, the Germans look with some contempt, as behind the age. So far they have considerable reason. If we must choose, I would sooner have our faith than their knowledge—but if possible a combination of both."

Concerning the professors and authorities of the place, he writes that they had "displayed uniformly the greatest politeness and kindness." But their politeness did not prevent his being amused with some of the adjuncts of a professor in that country, as compared with matters of that sort which had been familiar to him in his own.

"The German professors have most of them faces parched and cured by much smoking. and live entrenched within a multitude of doors. You call—find no one—go through various antechambers and folding doors—and at last, tapping at a door you suppose the right one, are told to walk in, and behold a man, in a sort of dressing gown, without a neckcloth, amidst a chaotic waste of books, who turns out to be the celebrated Dr. So-and-so, author of &c. &c."

My son highly valued the theological lectures of Professor Müller. He was grateful to Professor Tholuck, on many grounds, for his friendship. He spoke also in terms of admiration of a "long-locked orientalist" friend, whose "lingual treasures" were in his estimation not only of vast extent, but of great worth. In short, the pictures of German life which passed before him in those days never ceased to be objects of interest with him. Here is one of them :—

"*December* 21*st*, 1846.—Halle. . . . Some days ago, a student died here. He was about twenty-two, reading for the law; his disorder a nervous fever. Yesterday he was buried, and the spectacle was certainly an imposing one. A white coffin of carved wood, ornamented with wreaths, and with the cross swords laid on the top, was borne on the shoulders of men in long black cloaks and cocked hats; then followed a band playing solemn music; then a long train of students, the seniors of the student corporations, with their drawn swords, white gauntlets, white scarfs, and plumes in their caps; and in the rear a small body of the volunteer troops. When we came to the grave, the swordsmen surrounded it in the first row, and Tholuck, who was there in his gown and doctor's cap (exactly like the pictures of Martin Luther), gave a short address. Among other things, he said—'The grave is but a little hill, yet from it how small do the great affairs of life look—how great the small!' As the coffin was lowered, the instruments sent forth some of the saddest, softest, most sweetly melancholy tones I ever heard. We then sang, all of us, a few words—the clods were thrown upon the coffin, and the ceremony was over. There was something to me inexpressibly mournful and beautiful about the whole scene which I shall never forget. The student here is not buried as every one else is buried, but with an honour peculiar to himself. But I wondered where his soul was, and thought of the sorrow of those to whom he was dear."

Soon after my son had entered upon his studies at Halle, a literary project took possession of his mind, which he was prepared to work out in a manner so earnest as to cause me some anxiety. He knew that his pulpit services had been generally acceptable. He was aware that his sermons, while containing much to interest the intelligent and the thoughtful, contained much also which the humblest and the poorest had been disposed to treasure up as very precious. But he could not bring himself to think that he had the force, the pathos, or the readiness which seemed to be so necessary to anything beyond an average success in the pulpit. At the same time he could not conceal from himself that it was possible for him to do something much above the average doing of men of his class and age. He felt also, that it seemed to belong to the nature which God had given him that he should look to mental effort—to the surmounting of difficulty, in order to the realization of his conceptions in some form of efficient and useful authorship, as to the great charm of life. In so far his tendencies were in the main according to my wishes. But it was a matter of deep regret with me that he could not look forward to service in the pulpit more hopefully Several circumstances combined to fill him with discouraging thoughts in this respect. He was well aware that the congregations he would be called to address would be mostly intolerant of the preacher who must read his sermons, and that his shortness of sight disqualified him for reading to advantage, even were reading permitted. His memory, at the same time, was not of a sort easily to recall words. When he had been at the pains of writing his sermons, he could scarcely deliver a sentence as he had written it. He was thus shut up, so far as language was concerned, to the alternative of either reading entirely, or extemporizing entirely. If the speaker who must always repeat his language from memory can hardly be expected to rise to great eminence as an orator, the same may be said of the man who can never avail himself of premeditated words, but must always depend for them on the moment. Had my son entered on his career as a preacher only a dozen years later, he would probably have been allowed to read in the pulpit, and as he would have been able by that means to ensure the exact enunciation of what he wished to say, he might have been led to concentrate his strength on his pulpit discourses, and have left us many finished compositions of that order, in place of much we now have from his pen. The man who can address an auditory from the pulpit as the senator has to address the speaker in the chair, or as the barrister has to address the twelve men in the jury-box, possesses a great advantage. But there are men who must be allowed to read, or they always fall below their own idea of how they should acquit themselves, and being dissatisfied for the most part with their best efforts, are liable to become disheartened in their work.

It should be added that my son's reasons for not regarding the sermon as a proper theme for elaborate effort extended to some other forms of composition. He began to look on periodical literature as coming very much under the same category with discourses from the pulpit. It appeared to him that the teacher from the pulpit, and the teacher from the periodical press, must necessarily have much to do with the fragmentary and ephemeral, and that this being known to be the nature of the work, the consciousness of this fact must be unfriendly to the highest order of effort on the part of the workman.

Of course it is no sin for a man to have a passion for literature. Having the passion, it can be no sin to be desirous of doing the best that may be done by him in that walk. In this there may be ambition, but the ambition may be virtuous. My son's feeling in relation to periodical literature was not peculiar to him. Many minds of his complexion have so felt. Every one must know that what is done in periodical publications, is done to a large extent for the hour, and passes away with the hour. The personal sacrifices made by many who labour in this field for the sake of great public interests, are little understood by the multitude. It is not difficult, accordingly, to understand how it comes to pass that so many literary men rarely touch literature of this description, and that the ablest writers in such publications are generally careful so to write that their productions may admit of being republished. The confession is thus made, that without this prospect of permanence, the requisite stimulus for doing their best would be wanting. It is observable, too, that men who have their season in which they contribute brilliant papers to reviews, by degrees seem to grow weary. The time comes in which they feel the want of a new impetus. They turn to something which they may elaborate more thoroughly, and deal with as being more truly their own. The period arrives, accordingly, in which they make their bow to Mr. Editor, on the plea of being about to set up business for themselves. Shall we censure such renegades? Before we do so, let it be remembered that in this class of delinquents we find such men as Lord Macaulay and Sir James Stephen. Even Sydney Smith, whose elastic genius did immensely more than that of any other man to *make* the *Edinburgh Review*, began at length to drop his pen, and to plead excuses.

My son's letter from Halle which has suggested these remarks, apprized me of his intention to do something with the great men, and the great epochs, of Church history. But he was not content to treat such topics in prose. His taste both for poetry and history were regarded by him, as we have seen, as a sacred gift, for the best use of which it became him to account himself as religiously responsible. His intention, for this reason, was to write a series of dramas, each on some great ecclesiastical name, and on the age with which that name is associated. The series, when complete, was to embrace the most remarkable phases of Christian history from the beginning. Some of my readers will remember that the first conception of the *Paradise Lost* presents it, not as a succession of books, but as a succession of dramas. It does not appear that my son was at all influenced by that fact in giving to his project a historico-dramatic complexion. The following passage from one of his letters to a friend will best show what his conception was:—

"I have thought more and more of the plan concerning which I spoke to you in my last, and it appears to me, considered from all sides, and considered with all earnestness, to be, so far as I can now judge, the thing I seem to have been meant to do. The display such dramas would afford of the inner working of the religious feeling in various characters and circumstances, and the chapters in our mental history which it would unfold, would, if I should do my subject justice, be no less full of instruction than of interest. The fierce mental agitation of the men converted as it were by a divine force from great wickedness to great holiness; the mistaken enthusiasm of the fanatics; the manly devotion of the heroically good; the aspirations of the martyr after his crown; the gentler emotions of the heart—the tenderest love of the mother, the sister, or the wife, brought into the midst of the conflict of the rude iron times of ages past, and swept away in a common desolation; the downward progress of a soul once partially enlightened, but falling away farther and yet farther; the joy of fiends and the sorrow of angels over it; the struggles of that soul itself against the coiling of the worm that dieth not which it already begins to feel closer and yet closer—all this would be replete with tragic lessons, of the fairest, loveliest, and most fearful import. Much deep thought—heartsearching—prayerful studying of the soul's depths—much patient and wide reading and investigation—much felicitous invention would be required. Yet I see nothing else in which I could so unite my will and God's, and be serving him in the way towards which I feel the greatest impulse. Man's applause may come or not as it will. My concern in it will be over when the last stone has been laid—when the last line has been written."

. . . . .

This is a magnificent sketch. But my exceptions to the scheme were many, and, I believe, weighty.

The following extract from a letter in reply to them, will further disclose the writer's thoughts on the subject, and something of his state of mind generally at that time :—

"I am sure you cannot think that self-will, or a conceited confidence in my own opinion has anything to do with my resolve in this matter. You know that in general I have been too ready to submit to the opinions of others my equals, rather than to impose mine upon them. But the thing is, I feel that it is high time for me to be doing something *definite.* Here am I, not far from four-and-twenty, and up till very lately no preponderating aim anywhere. Sometimes theology—often preaching—often prose writing—often poetry, have been successively my favourites—or, rather, have been all favourites together. But in *all* these it is not for living man to succeed. The men who have done much have been men who have early decided on some one thing that they would set about and carry through. The men who have done nothing, and might have done something, are those who, like —— and ——, have been reading, and musing, and laying a general foundation of miscellaneous information, and writing *bits* of things, but who have never braced themselves to some real effort, and looked steadily forward to a distant completion. Up to the present time, my efforts have been as uselessly divided among a multitude of pursuits as they were in England. The only difference has been, that they have been all German, instead of being all English. But this will lead to nothing. If I were to suffer this to continue, I should return to England with another language certainly, and increased information, and enlarged views, but with no step taken to rescue me from the fate of those whose life is a thing of fragments. I must decide now, or I never shall. The fatal habit will be contracted of only doing such things as a few sittings may complete—many sketches in water-colours, nothing more enduring. I might write a few articles in the *Review* on German literature and German philosophy—perhaps I might make them interesting—people would be pleased for an hour or two, but there the thing would lie. I might get the credit for writing articles with spirit and smartness, but as I shall never make a philosopher, it would be nothing more than a superficial handling of the subject. It would not be anything I could follow out so as to be able to say I have done *that*. Your own course was quite of another sort. You did not spend years upon preliminaries, but when not much older than I am, grappled with so great an undertaking as the life of Wycliffe itself. . . . Most of the successful competitors in all the avenues of life have decided on something to which they would devote the main part of their energies before they came to my time of life. If I wait longer, my life, instead of going out like a cannon-ball direct to its mark, will be ignominiously dribbled through a sieve.

"So far, then, concerning the necessity of some fixed aim at once. This, and more than this, I have thought at different times, in many different forms. Then comes the question—*what?* Here I have seriously considered what the tendency of my past life has been—to what, on the whole, it has been most constantly turning—what its advantages have been—what I feel at this present time most desire for doing, and also what wants doing. And so in my love for poetry, and my interest in the development of the truth, and the dealings of God in the history of his Church, I find the two elements which, put together, make the work on which I should feel the utmost toil a pleasure. These two preferences constitute, I think, the qualifications for such a work, if I only use them conscientiously and resolutely.

"To preaching—*though I love it from my soul*, for its own sake and the sake of others—I should not be justified in giving myself *wholly*. That, indeed, I ought to do, but not to leave the other undone. If I had been intended to do any great work as a preacher there would have been signs of it, and I should long ago have thrown aside all other pursuits. With regard to prose writing on theological subjects I know of nothing I could write that would satisfy me. A doctrinal work could be far better written by numbers than by me. A work on some period of the history of the Church, or of opinion on theological subjects, I could write with much interest, but not the highest. In the wilderness of prose I should have too many remembrances of the lost paradise of poetry. . . .

"I see not how I can consistently write any prose, even for the *Review*, while engaged as I propose, for it will require a diligence and determination as great as your own to make preaching compatible with this other labour, and it would be impossible to carry on that *and* prose writing together. At all events, I shall publish the dramas, either separately or in groups of two or three, and not wait till the whole design is complete. Should I find my offering utterly rejected, I shall have at least the consciousness that I did not miss one of the greatest and best things to which a man could apply himself, from the want of courage to make the attempt. The labour itself will give me a far deeper satisfaction than any fame, concerning which I strive to be more and more indifferent. I shall commence the series with Savonarola. I think it will not be necessary to pay regard to chronological order in the order of composition. I may afterwards take up Chrysostom, perhaps Hildebrand, endeavouring in all not merely to develop the character of the principal personage, but to give an exact picture of the religion and political spirit of the times. They must be dramas on the principles of *King*

John or *Henry IV.*, rather than on those of *Hamlet* or *Macbeth.* It is now a quarter to eleven, an hour for retiring to rest which I very seldom exceed.

Your affectionate Son."

After citing the above extracts, it is due to the writer of this letter to allow him to state for himself his views concerning the nature of poetry and the mission of the poet. In a paper written by him a few months before are the following passages :—

"According to some critics, the great office of poetry would seem to be to exalt the common and the low. In their view its effects would resemble those of the mirage, under which the houses and oxen on the dead level of some savannah appear to be raised in various attitudes into the air. Given a certain amount of the prosaic, the question is, how much poetry can be extracted from it? The more apparently hopeless the task, the greater the glory of success. The verse-maker who, on this principle, offers us a sorry leaf instead of the true poetic fruit, would have us always remember, in alleviation of our disappointment, how very far he had to go to fetch it, and how wonderful it is that any vegetation at all should be found in the region from which it came. The error is, that such labour is but busy idleness after all.

The great difficulty—that of producing great poetry—is avoided altogether. It is as though a painter should bend all his efforts to produce an accurate representation of the gloss of silks and satins, to the exclusion of any attempt at original design, or any study of the true principles of his art. A conquest over a self-imposed difficulty, whether arising from the nature of the subject or any needless complexity of rhyme or metre, is not to be substituted for victory over the real difficulty with which the poet is beset. The heroes of this order of poetry are entitled to equal praise with the French versifiers of the fifteenth century, who rejoiced in the rigme batelée, *rigme brisée*, *rigme empesière*, &c., or with that unfortunate monk who composed a volume of hexameters on the Virgin, consisting of transpositions of the words, 'Tot, tibi, sunt, virgo, dotes, quot, sidera, cœlo.' The true aim of poetry will be realized in this way so soon as those sages immortalized by the veracious Captain Gulliver shall have succeeded in extracting sunbeams from cucumbers. Poetry suffers by such attempts, and the subject gains nothing. The hapless poet (alas! that he is no eagle), powerless as the crow to lift the sheep upon which he has pounced, sticks fast in the wool.

"The thoughts of poetry, star-like, should be about it. The great poet does not spend life in executing microscopic copies of the small parts of nature. He makes the universe the scaffold for his ideal. He fills the world with thoughts on pilgrimage to build shrines of his own, as well as to visit those which time has consecrated. It is the office of his art, not merely to show to the mind its workings, to hold up to the reader a reflection of his own feelings, but also to display before him things that by no other means could be revealed—wonders of which otherwise he would never have dreamed. Hence its power to ennoble and instruct. To cut off from poetry this, its high province, is to confound it with metaphysics, and to convert it into the genius which wields the dissecting knife in place of the flaming sword. Metaphysics shows man what he is—poetry, what he is, and what he should be. The one classifies his powers, the other educates them. The poet not only portrays nature, but strives after an ideal excellence, not contrary to, but combined from and founded on that which is real. While limning the earth fairly, he carries us to imagined regions beyond it, measures mortal capabilities, not only as they are, but as they will be, and shows us religion and virtue somewhat as they appear in their own country, as well as here, in their less worthy place of sojourning. . . .

"Simplicity has assuredly much to answer for, owing to the numbers who have paraded their barrenness under her name. No doubt, it is quite true that needless and incongruous imagery is a blemish; but may it not also be true that he who professes to be so scrupulous in the use of it has made a virtue of necessity, and exhausted his whole store to supply us thus poorly; while the fertility of his more prolific brethren excites his censure, from reminding him but too keenly of the woful pains he has undergone in bringing to light the few thoughts he has himself produced? Some have carried this principle so far as purposely to exclude from their dramas all that is ordinarily termed poetry, as though it were impossible to become poetical without, at the same time, being undramatic. This is too much the case with the dramatic poems of Mr. Taylor. Such a rule looks so like the welcome announcement of tragedy made easy, as naturally to meet with a cordial reception from the less gifted members of the poetic guild. No careful student of human nature, or of Shakspeare, its truest mirror, will deny that metaphorical language furnishes the natural utterance of passion. . . .

"Epithets are to poetry what finishing touches are to a painting—if too numerous they give the performance an air of heaviness. In artistic phrase, they kill the lights. The well-chosen adjective, on the contrary, directs a ray to that particular part of an object which it suits the present purpose of the poet to bring out into prominent relief. Such descriptive terms are often alone sufficient to constitute poetry of a high order—as when Milton describes the evening star as 'the sleeping sea, with *handmaid* lamp attending ;' and Shakespeare's graphic expression, '*looped* and *windowed* raggedness,' is another example. Such words contain the subtilized essence of a refined comparison. Such concentration of similitudes, with their brevity and point, have a magic in them to penetrate the soul, powerful as that of the weird needles of the Swedish superstition which parted walls in sunder with a touch. . . .

"It is singular that those of our modern poets whose perceptions have been most deeply pervaded by the Grecian spirit should have departed so widely from it in the execution. Shelley, whose translations from the Greek are the finest in our language, and whose creations, for the most part, are so eminently classical in their design, has yet overlaid them everywhere with a profusion of imagery, which, with all its richness, is frequently involved and abstract. His poetry resembles nothing so much as a Grecian statue set up in a Cathedral, and having its white surface strangely variegated by the crimson, green, and violet tints thrown on it from the painted window. Miss Barrett, who, in her *Vision of Poets* and *Dead Pan*, portrays, with a graphic force, like that of Æschylus, a succession of figures worthy of a place on the marble of some antique frieze, has greatly impaired the effect of some among her other poems by those peculiarities of diction which an apparent imitation of the great but immature genius of Keats has now-a-days rendered so prevalent."

It will be seen from these passages that the mind of the writer was becoming rapidly alive to the distinction between the use and abuse of imagery in poetry. We have a right to conclude, that verse from his pen in 1846, when these paragraphs were written, would have been a great improvement, in respect of clearness and chastened simplicity, on the poetry published by him only two years before. The following passage from the same paper, though somewhat long, should not be omitted in this place :—

"It has ever been a part of the province of imagination to bridge with its rainbow those spaces which science has failed to fill up with any certain knowledge. But if it be true, that the more we know the more we discern the extent of the unknown, there can be no reason to fear that the triumphs of science will really diminish the domain of the poetical. These two sources of influence, like the spiritual and providential dispensations of the Divine Being, are formed to work in separateness, but not in hostility. Time, while opening to us many of the doors of mystery, points to yet more beyond them, of which he still holds the key.

"The poet's great work should be done 'unto God.' When this is the case, his occupation is, without exception, the highest upon this side heaven. To his faith in religion, faith in this fact should be added. The poet, in his Paradise, like Adam in his, has a right direct from God to give names to the creatures—not without ever and anon an upward glance for aid that he may name aright. But only in poetry is it possible to write adequately concerning the poet. The defence of poetry, however, may well be left to the humbler efforts of prose.

"It is said that poetry is of no practical utility. From those who look at things in so utilitarian an aspect as to see nothing more in the sun than a central hinge for the mechanical forces of our system, or a huge stove whereat the planets may warm their faces, such a verdict is not surprising. But this same sun has a higher, a moral, a religious utility; and this is the species of usefulness possessed by poetry. The mind most poetical is fitted to become the most religious. The poet and the Christian have alike a hidden life. Worship is the vital element of each. Poetry has in it that kind of utility which good men find in their Bibles, rather than such convenience as they have in their railway guides. It ennobles the sentiments, enlarges the affections, kindles the imagination, and gives to us the enjoyment of a life in the past, and in the future, as well as in the present. It cultivates those faculties within us, which the more we cultivate them, the more do we find meanness a thing impossible. From the elevation on which it places us, the steepness of the descent required for the deed of baseness appears in its true shame and peril. Under its light and warmth we wake from our torpor and coldness to a sense of our capabilities. This impulse once given, a great object is gained. The precise direction which this revived activity shall take, we learn as a subordinate branch of knowledge from a contemplation of ourselves and our particular circumstances. Thus Schiller has truly said, 'Poetry can be to a man what love is to the hero. It can neither counsel him, nor smite with him, nor perform any labour for him, but it can bring him up to be a hero, can summon him to deeds, and arm him with strength for all that he ought to be.'

"From a false estimate of the office of poetry in this respect, arises the error of those who would have the poet select everyday and domestic themes for his art. Thus Emerson, in one of his Essays, writes as follows: —'Our log-rolling, our stumps and their politics, our fisheries, our negroes and Indians, our boats, and our repudiations, the wrath of rogues and the pusillanimity of honest men, the northern trade, the southern planting, the western clearing, Oregon and Texas, are yet unsung.'

Alas! for the poets that are, or that are to be, if it is only by hanging their pearls upon shapes so uncouth that they are to secure their immortality. The poet sets before men the lesson which it is for them, not for him, to apply. A writer who should endeavour to eke out his own deficiencies by thus seeking to give his poem an interest and a power from extraneous sources which he himself was unable to impart, would bear no little resemblance to those Nestorian missionaries among the Tartars, who professed to cure diseases with holy water, but mistrusting the virtues of their panacea, thought it expedient previously to mingle rhubarb with the large draughts of the sacred element they prescribed.

"The poet makes man wiser by causing truth to speak to him in a language that appeals to his whole nature, not merely to a part of it, and which reaches the heart as well as the intellect. Taught by him, we render it filial love as well as filial obedience. He makes man better, too, by revealing as none else can do, the native loveliness of generosity and patriotism, affection and self-sacrifice. It is no fair argument to urge that many poets have fallen short of such precepts in their practice. Truth and beauty are not changed by the imperfection of their human advocates. If some have been 'like diamonds cut with their own dust,' such fate, while mournful for themselves, has ever been among the most memorable of lessons for others. The very monument posterity sets up perpetuates the warning as well as the glory. The failure of the undistinguished has its teaching for a few. But when the hero falls, all eyes are upon him. It is not before the dismantled hut, but when gazing on the ruined temple, that we feel with most solemnity the frailty of man. Poetry does much also to increase our happiness by keeping alive within us those early feelings of love and confiding faith which a life of contact with the world tends so commonly to extinguish. It prevents the heart from growing old with the body, and like Idunna's fragrant apples, whose taste preserved the gods of Valhalla from old age, renews within us a divine youth."

Such were my son's views concerning the function of the poet in 1846. And it will, perhaps, be manifest to the reader that in these prose passages there are considerable indications of cultivated perception in relation to that art. But the writer is still intent on becoming a pastor and a preacher. Of preaching he can still say, "I love it from my soul, for its own sake and for the sake of others." He is quite alive, also, to the danger of allowing a love of fame—the passion so common with the poet—to become his guiding purpose. His great pleasure, he states, would lie in the sense of having done something in the face of difficulty which it would be good and beautiful to do. It is not needful to enter upon any defence of such aspirations. The desire to give form and reality to the good and beautiful may have respect to the good of others quite as much as to our own. In this view, the feeling under consideration may spring from benevolence more than from egotism, from generosity more than from selfishness. The Creator Himself makes the created to participate in the pleasure of his work. We are wont to conceive of him as happy in the contemplation of such reflections of his own happiness. And surely it may be permitted to the creative genius of man to find pleasure in the thought of extending delight kindred to its own to the distant and unborn. It is clear, accordingly, that there are conditions of the purest benevolence which are inseparable from what men call ambition. Power, eminence, influence, may be earnestly coveted, but it may be from a desire of the gratification to be found in the consciousness of having done something to diffuse the peaceful, the pleasurable, and the elevating.

According to the measure of a man's human feeling will be his indisposition to be divorced from humanity—his solicitude to be felt in its midst as an influence for good. The manly makes us to be at one with man. The love of fame for its own sake is simply a love of self; but we may shrink from the thought of being forgotten by our species from a sincere love of them; and we may covet power in order that the pleasure possible to ourselves from that source may be a pleasure imparted by our means to others. It may sound like a paradox, but it is a fact, that the most ambitious men are often the least selfish, while the non-ambitious are most so.

On these grounds, I was not disposed to deal harshly with my son's purposes and hopes, as set forth in the letter cited. They were, in some respects, disappointing to me. But it is with youth as with the newly-loosened carrier pigeon, which, from its high and strange place in the air, glances and darts right and left, before seeing the looked-for landmark, and rushing off on its intended track. Nor are the projects which in this stage of our experience seem to be failures really such. In ways too subtle for our foresight, they contribute to qualify us for doing the work which is ultimately given us to do. We rough-hew many things in our young and hopeful days, and what we finish at last is, perhaps, finished the better by the help of such preliminary practice. My impression was, that this contemplated series of ecclesiastical dramas would never see the light. But I had little doubt that something cognate would come, and would draw to itself a good deal of the spirit proper to the sort of compositions which were not to come.

While the mind of the student was fascinated by the visions described, a current of a very different kind was given to his thoughts. Nothing came to my knowledge at the time in regard either to the piety or orthodoxy of my son to cause me to regret his residence in Germany. But I have since been made aware that the mental atmosphere of Halle, and in some measure, probably, the complete separation to which he was there subject from those genial and domestic relationships in which he had grown up, was not favourable to his religious peace. His mind fell under the influence of a vague spiritual restlessness, discontent, and gloom. It resembled, in some respects, the experiences through which he had passed in Lancashire, but it was in other respects different. It came from larger views of the mystery of our existence, and embraced many more sources of misgiving and sorrow. There are passages in his letters at this time, especially to the loved one who afterwards became the partner of his life, and who lives to mourn his loss, which disclose to us something of the troubled region through which he then passed.

"*November*, 1846.—I scarcely know how the days go by. I live mentally like the earth, ever turning, now in light, now in shadow; at one time doing much, at another seeing so much to do that I do nothing; forming many plans of books—cobweb-fancies—mere brain-spinning, as the Germans call it; imagining sometimes our future life, and tossed on tumultuous feelings, waves of all sorts, and sizes, and strengths, and brightness, and darkness, with only the most distant possible sight of the haven caught only at intervals. And the thought fails not to come (how far just or not let the experience of every one decide), does not this shifting of shadows, and alternation of fears, and hopes, and restlessness, and vague aspiring, and despondency equally vague, does it not all come from the desire after happiness? And if a man could cease to wish to be happy, would he not be happy that instant? At least with a certain sort and fashion of happiness, but a something well worth having as the world goes, and which many a pining, downcast wretch would rejoice to obtain. It is not the true—that is in heaven—it is a graven image of it, however—an emanation, a picture, and what more can we expect? Therefore, the question, How may I be most happy? is sin, and comes to the same thing as, How may I be most wretched? In the search after the greatest good lie the seeds of the greatest evil. Some such philosophy might a solitary make, having a cavern on the sea-shore, and to whom the gloomy grandeur of the waves had imparted something of their own nature. Such a philosophy must a man alone at some time make for himself, to whom the outer world is the rocky cave, with its mere crust and water; and his own soul, with its limitless desires, its heaving commotion, or its deceitful slumber, the sea. Is not truth more likely to come to man's mind in converse with itself, and the truth about and above itself, than in company with his fellows? Let any one take out the viper selfishness from his bosom which has been warmed there so long (and if some of the heart comes away with it, let him not heed it), and let him, standing in the midst of change, and love, and hatred, say, none of these things move me—they may come or go, they are the accident, not the essence of my nature; and let him regard all about him as not concerned with himself—shut his eyes quite to his own little, contemptible, and soon-to-be-forgotten earthly career, and say, 'What will happen to me I know not—what comes I care not—this only I know, that, whatever happens to myself, there abides the holy which I worship—the beautiful, unchanged, undiminished, whether I am happy or wretched. There are fellow-creatures to be served, and served they shall be, perhaps by me, certainly by some. I love them, and, if permitted, will bless them.' Would not such a man have come to a great pass, even the *out*passing of the fretful and feverish desires that torment most of us? He would neither pine after fame, nor joy, nor love, but he would be love—he would be absorbed in what was beyond himself—he would lose his own identity in affection, in longing to be one with the purposes of God, to be a part of the building God's providence and grace build up: whether a stone near the foundation, dark, beneath the ground, in affliction or obscurity, or nearer one of the glorious pinnacles in the sunshine and light of men, it is not his concern, it is God's—some must be down beneath, and if that place God sees best for him, there he would soonest lie.

"It might appear that such notions lean too much toward the quietism of some of the French Catholic writers; but yet when a man sees but a few fathoms into the pit of darkness, namely, his own heart, it becomes sober verity. This is not German philosophy

—my reading has been lying lately another way; but this is how my own thoughts turn themselves, and work themselves, and keep me waking at night, and haunt me in the day time. So I write as I am now thinking. But you will say such views of life lead to indifferentism —bring a frosty winter into life's very spring, and pull it to pieces as completely as you used to do our flowers. Exactly, I reply, the thing required—indifference—that is, to pull to pieces our own flowers for ourselves, to have no set form and shape of life-happiness which we will choose and have for our own, and say, I will have that or nothing, like a child with its toy. Then, and then only, are we free, and at least not so unhappy as we otherwise should be."

"*November 27th*, 1846.—Pour moi, physically I am well, metaphysically no great things; it is such very hard work to keep out of a universal disgust of existence. It is a perpetual driving on a lee-shore, and no rounding the cape. Life becomes a sort of dolorous delight and magnificent misery; I know not what else to call it. The past is a garden with so many flowers that the nourishment they draw for their support takes all the moisture and productive power from the barren soil of the present: the future—that you know I always regard rather as a precipice than as a land of Beulah—a thing which, as it is not, may never be. If the past is not a torment, the future ought not to be a delusion. Take away the past and the future, and what is the present? A season wherein, when we do think, we are unhappy; when we do not think, unwise. Verily, threescore years and ten of this sort of thing ought to content any man. Every winter should come to each, asking him at the close of the year, 'Well, have you not had enough of it now?' And man stands up with his sins and his sorrows, his unsatisfied desires and contemptible aspirations, and thinks himself a hero because he can say 'No!' Every drowning kitten would say as much if it could speak. It is not heroism, only instinct. In overcoming the instinct there is certainly heroism. I never could understand that natural shrinking which theologians and casuists alike unite in saying a man must feel at the prospect of annihilation. They say that the thought rubs the soul against the grain, that it flies in the face of the first principles of our nature—that to believe in ceasing to be, must be, till you do cease to be, the utmost misery. I cannot perceive it. The reason for what they say is, I conceive, in the mistake that they imagine the soul as existing *after it has been annihilated*, and as regretting its own annihilation—that they cannot separate the idea of annihilation in their minds from that of an after-consciousness which shall be affected in some manner thereby, seeing that annihilation cannot be unpleasing to the annihilated, for there is no annihilated at all when he has been annihilated. So much for people's ideas on the subject. . . . I wish I could see in Scripture good reason for believing in the annihilation of the lost.

"*Dec. 3rd.*—Life goes on with its succession of nights and days, and the perpetual rising and falling of the scales of light and of darkness, somehow. Time goes, and we go with it, but scarcely knowing how. To live is, to me, like being led blindfold through the streets of a great city—a confusion of sounds, the bustle of feet, and the rolling of vehicles—a sensation that some parts are lighter and others darker, that in some places the pavement is less smooth, in others more so—the crying and the laughing of children on either side, and the hum of the traffickers—the buyers and sellers of varieties—and that is all. It is of no avail to ask where we are. The conductor is a mute. We can only wait till the bandage shall be taken off our eyes: that will be when we can go no further. Then will the opened eyes be dazzled in a palace, or horror-struck by the sights that shall meet them in the eternal lazar-house—the hospital of sick souls for ever cureless. If a man says he has a purpose, it avails him nothing. He thinks he moves towards it, and hastens as though he were in the right way; yet he cannot be sure that he has not chosen a wholly wrong path. We may fall back for refuge on our motives, and say, come what will, I *mean* well. But even of that, with the strange mixture of which we are composed, there is no certain judging. Many have said so in their hearts, and yet in their lives done evil, and served Satan when they thought they were serving God. How unspeakably important that we should have some data whereby to go. Yet what are such, and where to be found? A most happy thing truly to hear a voice where the roads part, 'This is the way in which thou shalt go.' But who can be sure as to *whence* the voice comes? We desire guidance, but we cannot know if we have it. We profess to cast aside our own will, but in the very moment have we our bias on one side or the other. A preponderance of motive this way or that—this grows and decides us—and we imagine we are directed. What is it but our own will, our own inclination, that is all the time active? Ask what we will, we feel it is *we* who must decide. To feel the importance of our actions paralyses action. We estimate the consequences somewhat to us and to others of the steps we take, and the very revelation of what human activity really is makes us fear to act. We are told not to be careful concerning the morrow—that cannot mean that we should not weigh well the steps we take in life—that we should not task our judgment to the utmost to act as will be best; and yet, when we do so, what does it avail when our knowledge is so circumscribed—when our self-deceptions are so many!

"But why do I trouble you with these reflections?

Why perplex you with my perplexities, and write what might tend to throw over life, in your view of it, the same gloom which it increasingly possesses in my own? The truth is, that such thoughts are at present *myself*, and if I did not write them, it would be some other who wrote and not I. There comes the necessity for writing as I am. While it is the necessary consequence of solitude, of which I am now almost wholly the captive, to feed the soul on the bread and water of sadness, to make a tumult of fearful noises about the dungeon to scare away sleep, and to cause imaginations to become realities: with those whose life is happily passed in more of social activity these phantoms have no existence. The consequence is so natural, that I have scarcely reason to complain. Every man left alone, who thinks to any purpose, must turn his thoughts inwards on himself. But, so doing, he must find there much that grieves and repels him. He begins to hate himself. Self-contemplation, the holy sister of selfishness, makes him, through a selfish process, hate that very self. But can any man really hate himself? A man may say he does—do we ever really do so? Scarcely. I think it more true to say that we *despise* ourselves; we love ourselves always, but self-contemplation, introspection, fills us with contempt for that which is still and necessarily dear to us."

Reader, hast thou never known anything of the self-contradiction, the processes of self-torture, in which spirits become skilled which descend into these depths of spiritual life—or rather spiritual death? It is not certain that exemption from such dark hours should be accounted a matter for congratulation. Many, no doubt, ascend to heaven without ever descending into regions which seem to be so far away from it. But such souls do not go to the highest heaven. Nor will they ever be able to show others the road thither. The men who find beyond others their all in God, are the men who have known beyond others what it is to be without Him—to feel after Him and not to find Him. We must look down thus deeply into the confusions of the present, and up into the harmonies of the future, as such spirits in bygone times have done, before we can hope to understand what is meant by the passing of such natures from earth to heaven. Soon after the above passages were written, the writer of them was permitted to learn something of that transition from darkness into light which such tried ones know how to accept thankfully, as the precursor and type of the ascent into that state where the light is no longer mingled with darkness.

In January, 1847, my son thus writes:—

"The exhilaration of entering on the new space of time with reinvigorated hopes and efforts wherewith to fill it, has banished not a few gloomy thoughts; they are left behind and I see them no more. The wonderful profusion of mercies which were daily granted me during the year that is gone, though they increase the sense of my undeserving, speak of a Providential goodness that wakes up my thoughts to love and to gratitude. It is well to know ourselves, but such knowledge too exclusively is not good. If any would meditate more on himself, let him also meditate more on Christ, or the sight of the plagues of his own heart will rob him of all hope and consolation. So I have found it to my sorrow. We believe it, but experience alone can stamp the lesson deeply, that love to Christ is knowledge, and gratitude to Him wisdom, and that at the foot of the cross alone can we with safety reflect upon ourselves. Reasoning may make us believe, but the sense of guilt causes us to *feel* that Christ must be divine."

The following passage shows that the writer was not

prepared to admit in the retrospect that mere loneliness had been the chief cause of his late feeling of depression.

"*Jan. 8th.*—With the new year a new power seems to have come over me, whose serene influence I still continue to experience. There were seasons during the latter part of the past year in which I have suffered more unhappiness than in almost any past period of my life—not owing at all to home-sickness, or the depression consequent in some minds on the mere sense of solitude—but from a variety of causes which operated to fill my mind with darkness. Now all seems brighter, not with the sparkling of false hopes or fancy, but with the steadier light of truth and gratitude.

"*Jan. 28th.*—I cannot be sufficiently thankful that I feel at the commencement of this year so differently from what I did at the close of the last. Of the despondency that then as with a sort of supernatural power overcame me, I now feel nothing, and my spirits, though while in absence from you it is impossible that they should be elated, are yet in comparison tranquil. The quiet even progress of the days in regular study seems to have its correspondence in my own mind, and the contrast and conflict between the outer and the inner life no more agitates me. The faith which was overshadowed can once more behold her heaven, and the feeling of contentment, that much-prized blessing, does not disdain to visit me."

Minds which pass through such experiences, reserving them, as the subject of this memoir did, almost wholly to themselves, give evidence of sincerity. Not so the flippant class of sceptics who can chatter to the bystander about the difficulties of belief, so as to seem to say that the Almighty ought to feel surprised and obliged when any man of intellectual pretensions is found to believe in Him. If God has spoken at all, we may be sure He has so spoken as to make it simply reasonable that we should accept His utterances. What may be His reasons for withholding light for a season from honest and devout spirits we can know but in part. But we do know that the Christian Pilgrim was not safe against falling into the hands of Giant Despair, and being lodged in Doubting Castle. To Alfred, trial in this form never returned. I give an extract from one of two letters some months later, which will serve to show how such trials in the minister may be included in the discipline intended to qualify him for speaking the word in season to those who sit in darkness.

"What you say of —— in your last excites my heartfelt sympathy; and the more because I know those feelings only too well myself. I have felt what it is to be overmastered by the doubt that I had neither part nor lot in the matter—to wish many times a day that I had never been born, to water my couch with tears in the night, and to feel, as the Psalmist says, the pains of hell get hold on me. Though such seasons must be, in most cases, brought on by our own transgression—and that it was otherwise with me I would not say—yet the trial has had this result, that I can understand others in the same affliction as no man can who has not himself so suffered. And for the office to which I look forward how needful is such knowledge. At those times no promise is believed. This only is felt—that our God is a consuming fire. This only is heard—that He hath somewhat against us, and that somewhat enough to plunge us into everlasting perdition. We call on God, but how vainly? We weep, but they are tears of anguish and despair, not of contrition. How we envy the fowls of the air and the beasts of the field, and how gladly would we be relieved from the insufferable horror of immortality. When we feel that we must live for ever, and cannot hope, our sufferings approach those of the lost. But it is a mercy that such seasons, for the most part, must reach their climax ere long, after which the waters gradually subside; or else something comes from without, or springing up suddenly from within, sets the soul in a new position. It sees light once more, and looks at all things *in* that light. I could say much here, but the best comfort is summed up in the words (be they but well thought on) uttered by our Saviour on the cross, 'My God! my God! why hast thou forsaken me!' The sympathy of Him who said that we have. He knew, when He suffered for us, what it was to feel forsaken of God."

The letters of my son from Halle touch on a variety of subjects, and a few extracts from them will enable the reader to judge of the habit of thought which the young Englishman took with him to his studies. Touching on what it is that gives real value to life, he says:—

"Some men who have died young have lived far longer than others who have out-past their three-score years and ten. Life consists not in the abundance of things a man possesseth, nor in the abundance of things a man doeth, but in the abundance of thoughts he thinks, leading towards some special result, be that result in this world or the next. If we measure life by thought, how short will it be for most of us! How many years must we strike out of it! We must be content to be children. We are humbled at once. The pride and glory of the human mind in the abstract vanishes before a single dispassionate examination of the real employment of that mind. This very consequence shows that such a measure cannot be very far from the right one. If we believe that self-love is ever ready to present the standard that would set us highest, we should encourage the testimony which would set us lowest. The bias must be avoided by a movement to the opposite extreme. It is easier to act than to think. That we have not thought enough must be the burden of our lament at every retrospect. It is the refrain of the dirge over our ruined hopes and crumbling resolutions. The more we think, the more we shall do. The thought that leads to no action is not thought, it is dreaming. Sometimes our very diligence arises from our aversion to think. One man avoids thought by gaiety, another by study, both procedures being dictated by cowardice. But it is better to act without thinking to some purpose, than neither to think nor act. Yet why should we not think more than we do? It is so difficult. Difficult, however, only from want of practice. We need not be all thought. We are not all soul—we must be thought and action, as we are soul and body.

The thought which has *brought us to certainty* about some motive or purpose will last us a long time, perhaps through the entire carrying out of such purpose. This is the right use of thinking. For instance—we are no longer as a wave of the sea, driven about and tossed, when we are assured that our wish is to live to God; when we attain the conviction that Christ is the central point of our being, that we do what devolves upon us, that we bear what afflicts us as *His*. To be our own is to be full of anxiety. To be His, is to cast all our care upon Him."

The writer's letters from Halle abound in thought of this complexion, which will probably remind the reader of John Foster, more than of any other English author. But this more weighty cast of observation is interspersed with literary criticism of a lighter kind. The following on Spenser may be taken as a sample.

"From Spenser's 'Faëry Queen' you perhaps expected another order of beauty than that for which it is admired, and so were, as I was somewhat at first, in a measure disappointed. But it will be only at first; I think you cannot fail at last to relish him. Not that you need read all through. So exclusive a study would for you be waste of time. There are few parts superior to what he has in the cantos of the first book. If you read that twice or thrice, and give yourself up to the exquisite fancy of the pictures and the music of the inimitable stanza, I think you will be sensible of the fascination of that tender romantic sweetness for which he is distinguished. His almost feminine gracefulness, and the soft beauty of his imagery, beguiles, but does not startle. It is a gentle river, not a mountain waterfall. And so I think he has been a greater favourite with our sex than with yours. We luxuriate in the day-dreams of the enamoured poet, and become ourselves in love with the heavenly Una. But as we love what contrasts with us by gentleness, and is the opposite of our ruggedness, so you love what contrasts with your softer nature by its force and power. Hence it is that military men are so fortunate with the ladies; and this made Desdemona love the fearless and adventurous Othello; and hence also the masculine and stormy Byron has been read by ladies from one end of England to the other; dull Spenser, a nature so akin to their own, has been forgotten. To this it should be added that winter is not the best time for reading Spenser—it should be under a tree in a wood in June. And lastly, it is necessary to forget that it is an allegory, and to believe all true in fancy."

What poetry became in his own hands at this time

may be seen in some verses addressed by a lover to the object of his affection.

To Eveline.

"The streamlet runs beneath the ice,
The seed lies hid beneath the snow,
The summer birds in summer lands
Await till winter rise and go.

And then the stream will wake to play,
And lay its icy armour by;
And spring will lift the mantle white,
And see her children where they lie.

The birds will sing anew the songs
Whose music winter would not hear,
And breeze to breeze with scent will say,
'I feel the summer coming near.'

But oh, my Eveline, my joy!
Whose love hath given my soul its flowers,
And whose are all the wingèd thoughts
That sing among its hidden bowers;

If thou should'st cease to shine and ray,
My love hath lit that earth in vain,

It bears no incense on its breast,
  But only thorns to give me pain.

My beams shall light some fairer orb
  To bear me richer fruits than these,
Where I may see my looks of love
  Reflected on less treacherous seas.

Ah! then my sunless heart would be
  In night and winter hopelessly,
And springs might breathe, and summers shine,
  But neither breathe nor shine for me.

A wandered world, a lightless star
  That turns, and nowhere finds its sun;
So must I love and so despair
  Until my weary course was run.

Oh, there may be who more deserve
  A love so full of bliss as thine,
But not a heart to which thy loss
  Could bring such anguish as to mine."

In poetry my son wrote nothing beyond a few verses while in Halle, though he wrote much relating to it. We have seen that with the opening of 1847 his speculative and religious perplexities had passed away. One effect of this better state of spiritual health was a determination to return to the plan of study which he had sketched for himself in his letter from Bremen. German philosophy was to be really studied after all. The letter to a friend, from which the following extract is taken, bears date Feb. 7, 1847 :—

"You will perhaps ask what can be occupying me so intensely? The fact is neither more nor less than this; that having had some conversation with Tholuck on the matter, I find from what he said that my difficulty with the philosophy must have been more in my attempt at it alone, without any assistance, than anything else. Of course, if there be a possibility of accomplishing the business, I would not willingly disappoint my father in the matter. Accordingly, I have renewed my efforts in going three times a-week to a man who fills people with philosophy on being filled with a large sum of money, and not without success. I have said nothing to my father about it, nor shall I till I have concluded the study, because I would rather surprise and please him by being able to show him what I have done, than by merely speaking of what I mean or hope to do. The immediate consequence is, that I feel myself congealing into prose very fast, and more full of arguments than of poetical fancies. Perhaps it will not be until summer that I can thaw myself back again into poetry. But the thing is useful, and I need the sort of balance furnished by a heavy mass of logical lumber. The more I think of the matter, the more I am convinced that it was with great reason that my father wished me to make myself acquainted with the philosophy of the age. That it is false and worthless I feel convinced, but its effects have been so momentous as to demand the attention of all thinking men. It is this philosophy, and this alone, which has reduced Germany to that state of general indifference to all that is essential to Christianity, in which no longer even a portion of it is found. It is true that the whole bent of my mind is so strongly set the other way—so much more full of love for art than for science—so much more disposed to admire a grand and beautiful production than a merely learned or argumentative one, as to deprive me of all inclination ever to write a philosophical work. But it is not less true that, as a part of mental education, such study will improve me; and that beyond this, it is only by thus entering the camp of the Danes, and, like my namesake, in the disguise of a minstrel, examining their positions for myself, that I can learn effectually to combat them afterwards. Such, in fact, is the great want of the age. With the strife between Dissenter and Churchman, Baptist and Pædo-baptist, I do not feel inclined to take part. But the great verities of religion, and whether we shall have a religion at all, or take philosophy instead, this is the true point of contest, and here the stand must be made."

During the remaining months of the session the writer continued a close student of German speculation. It was then that he laid for himself the foundation of that reasonable system of philosophy, as opposed to the sceptical and the mystical, which he employed with so much effect in after years. At the close of his severe labour in this direction, he thus writes:—

"*Feb. 28th*, 1847.—Our life may be divided into provinces which we travel through successively. The session here approaches its close, and I shall have reached shortly the limits—the border-territory of another of the life-counties. I have cut down on the way a considerable quantity of timber, that is, material wherewith good substantial household furniture may hereafter be constructed; but plucked, in verity, astonishingly few flowers; and in my course I have therefore scattered far more sawdust than pollen; a fact which may give rise to the doubt whether I shall ever have any natural flowers at all—whether they will not be all carved wreaths, and posies cut out of old oak, such as we may see in a gothic library. The review bears witness to very considerable powers of collection, but to very *in*considerable invention. That I have attained a nearer view, or even less, a more comprehensive survey of the realm of the Beautiful—of the imaginative land of Beulah, I can scarcely say. I have found no Delectable Mountains—I have found no shepherds with their telescope. But the matter being even thus, I have realized more perfectly the object for which I came hither than if it had been otherwise. I have to regret now and then misdirected effort—namely, the chopping with my hatchet at trees which, after all, were not cut down. But there is a maxim of Bacon's which I have laid up, and find to be a precious morsel of wisdom, namely, that when effort cannot be made to answer its primary aim, we should always take care that we have some secondary one for it. Certainly he is quite right. We have accumulated precious merchandize, and if the first ship does not carry it forth to realize its profit, we must find a second. If this maxim be observed, a man need lose next to nothing of his labour. It will be useful for *something*, if not for that which he intended. It is his wisdom to find such something; for he who reflects on the shortness of life, will see that he cannot afford to lose a single coin of what he has secured. It is thus that in looking back on the past in this light, I am anything but dispirited. With idleness, at all events, I have not to charge myself. I can see very little of what

I have done during the period that need be wholly loss —perhaps nothing, when one recollects the often unexpected usefulness of what had seemed utterly worthless. I think I see how the past has been a stage further of self-building. I am anxious to be, not what I wish to be, but what Christ would wish me to be. To labour for ourselves is a sorry task—to labour for *Him* the highest happiness. I think he would have me serve his cause so far as I may, on that side of it especially where lie the Imagination and the Feeling. Towards this I seem to have been more directed and fashioned. But the precise time, whether sooner or later, and the precise mode—in that I must be guided by circumstances, the requirements of the time, and so on. Having nothing of my own, may He save me from using what I have as though it were my own. If we had only ourselves to look to in these weighty matters, what an insufferable burthen would it be. But we can trust that His direction will not fail us."

CHAPTER III.

DAYS IN ITALY.

1847.

LEAVING Halle, Alfred made a pilgrimage to Wurtembergh, the Jerusalem of the German Protestants. He there saw the door—that is, where the door *was*—to which Luther nailed his Theses—trod the floor of the room in which he studied; paid due homage to the table before which he sat, and on which he wrote; gazed on a stone sculpture representing the four Evangelists writing the Gospels, executed after a design by the great Reformer; was privileged to see some much-valued manuscripts; also a piece of worsted, or rather silk-work, from the hands of Luther's wife, and a bust of the great man from a cast taken after death. Of course the spot where the Pope's bull was committed to the flames was not overlooked, nor the houses in which Melancthon and Cranach rested by night, and prosecuted their different labours by day.

But Wurtembergh was taken in the way to Berlin. In that capital several weeks were occupied in seeing great sights and great men. The curiosity of the humble but well-to-do couple in whose apartments my son found his lodgings, appears to have been much excited by his presence and manner. The lady, indeed, soon discovered that he must be a young lord. The husband, who wore a pair of enormous spectacles, came into the apartment with his pipe in his mouth, "to try the experiment of a little conversa-"tion, and asked if the people in England were all "*white?*" The writer adds that among the lower class of Germans "England is like the end of the world, "and an Englishman is almost as great a curiosity as "a man from the moon." In the same letter he writes, —"was last night in a society of literati, where I was "much interested, and saw some of the most celebrated "characters of Germany."

We regret that more concerning this visit to Berlin was not committed to writing. But a few weeks were expected to bring the visitor to England, when communication might be readily made in another form. The following brief notes are from his diary.

"On Saturday, went with Dr. Zumpt to a meeting of a scientific association, of which the Doctor was a member. A lecture was read which occupied scarcely three quarters of an hour. The reader was Link the botanist. He sat quite among the company, and frequently talked and entered into conversation in an easy and friendly manner. The subject of the lecture was the cultivation of the vine. It is evident that many of the scientific men of Germany are well acquainted with many languages—Hebrew for instance, and even Sanscrit. I saw Buch the geologist, Druve the meteorologist, and Rose the chemist.

"On Sunday, heard an admirable sermon from Höppen. On Monday, heard Neander lecture for two hours.

"Visited Schelling, an old man with hair white as snow, with large blue eyes, and a somewhat rotund face. Found him remarkably polite and gentlemanly.

"Thursday, dined at Zumpt's, where, among some other celebrities, I saw the Grimms. First Wilhelm, with his long dark hair arranged as we see in portraits of

Cromwell, and with dark eyes. His brother Jacob, redolent of German mythology and of German gramoratik, has hair perfectly white, and remarkable as curling like the hair of a child, all over his head. His eyes were blue and restless, his nose aquiline, in short, very like Goethe; and both had a most intellectual interest and poetical air about them."

It had long been my wish to cross the Alps, and to spend some months in Italy. In 1847 I found it possible to accomplish this purpose, and determined that Alfred should be the companion of my pilgrimage. Ample opportunity, as I thought, would then come for talking dispassionately concerning the future.

We left London in June, and did not return to England before October. We spent a week in Paris, which my son had not before seen. Leaving that place by Diligence, we reached by daybreak, on a beautiful summer morning, a height of the Jura mountains, which gave us our first view of the Alps. Rich were the tints of purple, and crimson, and gold, which threw their shadows over those far-off heights of everlasting snow! The moments in which we gazed for the first time on that distant vision were moments not to be forgotten. Geneva, and its neighbourhood, detained us some days. We then crossed the Simplon, and soon found ourselves at Milan. The months which followed were indeed a holiday season to both of us. We had traversed the Highlands of Scotland together some seven years before, but the scenery and associations of the Alps and the Apennines were of a higher order. We visited all the places of chief interest between Venice and Genoa in the north, and Naples and Pæstum in the south. We kept note books, in which record was made daily of sights and impressions. We might have written a book about our travels, with as much reason, perhaps, as many who have so done, but we felt that our passing from place to place was much too rapid to allow of our having anything to say to the public that could be really worth saying. We were, however, very far from thinking that our time in Italy had been wasted. On the contrary, we left that country conscious of having become possessed of a world of busy thoughts and emotions which could never have become ours apart from what we had there seen and heard. The travelled man may not be able to describe in exact terms what it is that travel has done for him, but its effects are not the less real, nor the less potent, on that account. Nor must the untravelled man hope to understand them. Travel never fails to make the wise man more tolerant of differences. It enlarges his feeling of brotherhood. In all that he has to do with man and his affairs, he is furnished with ampler materials for thought, and is prepared to form riper judgments, and to adjust himself to action with greater wisdom. To myself this branch of education came late, to my son it came in the right season. In the education of an intelligent and susceptible youth, it is not a small matter to have seen nature in the passes of the Alps, and from the slopes of the Apennines; to have traced the signs of a bygone power through the water-streets of Venice, or along the high-terraced palaces of Genoa; to have felt that our great dramatist has peopled the streets of Verona, and the road to Mantua after evening, with sights and sounds, as a genius like his could alone have peopled them; to have looked through the dim and thoughtful twilight on Bologna or Florence, and to have lived through the history which the sight of those cities is so fitted to recall; to have stood near the summit of Vesuvius, and to have seen its upthrown lava descend like a broken willow-tree of fire, pattering down the sides of its cone until they reach the foot of the traveller; to have sailed with Paul across the waters of Baiæ to Puteoli, the starting-point once for all wayfarers towards Rome; and in Rome itself, to have looked on those chains of hills which border the Campagna, so rich in historical memories, to have called back the men and the deeds of old while treading the greensward now covering the once beaten ways of the Forum Romanum, or to have gazed on that giant ruin, the Colosseum, under the light of the still and silent moon, shedding brightness on its projecting masses, and throwing its recesses into deeper shadow, where every distant footstep falls on the breathless quietude like the approach of some lingerer from the past, who must still haunt the desolations of the present—to have seen all this, to have felt thus, and greatly more of the same kind, was, in our estimation, an advantage of nameless value. The extracts which follow are selected from letters hastily written by my son during this period.

"*June 29th*, 1847, GENEVA.—From the windows of our hotel on the shores of the lake, we can see the white house where Byron lived, and likewise the trees of D'Aubigné's garden, very different links of reminiscence. This is the place for the forming and maturing of great thoughts—at Lausanne. Here Gibbon, Rousseau, and Byron and Shelley—here also Calvin, prepared themselves their immortality. I stood in the pulpit beneath the very sounding-board that had echoed the voice of the great Reformer, looked round on the church whereon he looked, and on the seats where once sat his auditors. That cathedral is to me a most hallowed spot, it is consecrated by genius that was consecrated to God.

"*July 3d*, MILAN.—Since I last wrote, we have been up Mount St. Bernard, experienced the rigours of the mountain climate to a very fair extent. On our way up, were befogged and benighted, and well-nigh lost our way in the snow of those desolate regions, all which was very romantic, but the refreshments wherewith the good monks resuscitated us were not less welcome. In the morning scraped acquaintance with the celebrated dogs.

Such a morning, so black, foggy, and miserable; among that ice and snow, nothing to be seen, but a polar climate felt after a tropical one. On our way down, the heat kept growing on us by a series of most grateful graduations. . . . From Brieg commenced the ascent of the Simplon—a winding road higher and higher up into the clouds. Majestic pines standing out against the deep blue of the sky on craggy summits—the distant line of the Bernese Alps—the Schonhorn, a vast snow-covered mountain, looking like an imperial throne hung with white; the streets, houses shut up, and falling to ruins. Then to Bologna, with its gallery and churches. The masterpieces of Guido are at Bologna. It is impossible to appreciate Paul Veronese without having been at Venice, or Guido without having been at Bologna. And now we are in Florence, the town about which history has so much that is interesting to say; where almost every form of government has at some time prevailed, and where the lights and shades, the good and the bad, have stood out each so strongly, so picturesquely, with such effect. . . . The night before last, we slept at a country inn on the top of the Apennines, and were awakened at midnight by a thunder-storm, the grandest I ever saw; we appeared to be in the very centre of it. The flashes of lightning were not now and then, but every other moment, and the thunder not so much in claps as a continual unintermitted roar, reverberated by the mountains on every side. It was a glorious sight.

"*July 30th*, GENOA.—We are now at Genoa, having arrived last night after a beautiful ride from Lucca, in point of *beauty* surpassing anything we have anywhere previously seen—such quiet bays of blue, and slanting hills of vine and olive. In the evening, the contrast of dark shadows and glorious glowing sunsets have formed a combination testifying with surpassing power to the fairness yet lavished upon earth. . . .

"*August 29th*, ROME.— . . . The mind fills so rapidly with new images; glimpses and corners of beauty are caught at every turn, and make their dwelling in the recollection; blue mountains behind trees, white columns seen against a distant hillside, a city at sunset, a distance seen through a dark avenue of trees—these in the mere point of natural beauty abound here, and of course the historical recollections, even where the object may be in itself uninteresting, are numerous enough. The old palace of the Cenci, with its gloomy deserted air, the house of Rienzi, the palace of the Orsini, the gardens of the Colonnas, are among the middle-age reminiscences to me most interesting. And then of classic spots there is no lack. Old imperial palaces turned into haylofts; and where the palace of Augustus stood, now a villa belonging to a Mr. *Smith*—changes enough. . . . I am in a sort of dreamy whirl with the number of such things of all possible descriptions— from the wonders of Raphael and Michael Angelo, to the stone absurdly said to bear the mark of our Saviour's feet. . . . I drank of the waters of the Egerian fountain, and beheld the so-called grove where the nymph or goddess favoured the Roman lawgiver at once with love and wisdom. In the distance was the temple erected to commemorate the spot where Coriolanus was turned from his purpose by the intercession of his wife and mother. The Baths of Caracalla are the finest remains of the sort; and the intricacy and hugeness of the fragments give an idea of the old magnificence, perhaps more even than the Colosseum."

The lines below were written in Rome.

The Colosseum.

O, Time, how many men, and works of men,
Hast thou abas'd beneath the flowers and weeds,—
Sowing Youth's green on Age's rottenness:
Heroes have been that did build round the world,
And from all sides did look down on't at the foot
Of their high selves and their fierce crowd of thoughts.
Rome's Colosseum silent 'neath the moon,
Is't not the type and image of all these,
Their stir of old, and their deep quiet now?

That the advantages of travel remain with you few

will deny. But it is no less true that its pleasures also are permanent. Its pictures are not merely pictures for the hour, they are pictures for life. They can be called back by the wand of the imagination with all the vividness of the past. The treasures thus acquired are treasures for all time. Many an event, by a subtle and involuntary law of association, will cause them to return, and with them the feeling of delight or wonder, and of old-world thought or new-world purpose awakened by them. As the wintry evening has come, and the snow has fallen, and the wind has rushed screaming around our dwelling, my companion in travel and myself have listened, and asked—how is it now on Mount St. Bernard? The old Hospice will need its thick walls on a night like this. Their shielding strength, and the flaring faggots on the hearth, must be welcome comforts in such a state of the elements. Poor monks, you should know how to look above the earthly, for an allotment like yours assuredly had no place in paradise.

So, when the sun has set with a special brilliancy, and sky and cloud have become gorgeous in crimson and gold, and all things over hill and dale, and over land

and sea, have blushed or brightened in answer to the marvellous colouring above them, at such moments we have said—Yes, this would be the sky under which to see old Spezzia once more, as we saw it at sunset, descending the winding road along the hill sides far above it, peering on our way into the purple, deep, and dark valleys stretching far down beneath us, and glancing upwards saw those far-off heights which, bathed in the fiery light of the departing day, became like crimson mists, while the nearer and richly graven mountain slopes were seen to be studded, from stair to stair in their descent, with village homes and knightly castles, all radiant in the glow of the Italian evening, as if to proclaim how Nature holds on her way with undiminished splendour, while ages of chivalry, and ways of men, come and go like the summer cloud. We could have filled many a page with reminiscences of this nature. But it sufficed to feel that we had them, and could never lose them.

The following is a description of the ascent of Mount Vesuvius :—

"Turning from the main road to ascend the hill, we soon reached the Hermitage, a sort of halfway house, where dwell two Franciscans, and a welcome entertainment is found for quadrupeds, if not for their owners. Then we started anew with our long working train—some eight or ten men, some carrying provisions, some cloaks, others waiting to bear the chairs in which the ladies were to be seated. Two armed soldiers accompanied us as an escort. Looking back as we ascended, the bay of Naples was seen in perfection; the sea, under the sunshine, was a dazzling sheet of blue and silver, the headlands sent down by the Apennines descending darkly to the edge of the waters. Off at the back of Naples lay an extended valley the Campagna Felice, where the Carthaginians became Lotophagi, and which is now the place of a becalmed fleet of towns and cities. On the other side, across the sea opposite to Naples, was Sorrento, and in the distance the beautiful island of Capri. About us were streams of lava which old eruptions had poured forth, broken in cooling into all sorts of shapes, sometimes like tangled ropes, or cables coiled together. Then the tremendous ascent of all but perpendicular dust, where by every step you seemed to lose more than you had gained. The exhaustion was extreme. It was a treadmill operation, such as I could hardly have imagined. At length we reach the summit, the great scoria plane which surrounds the inner cone. Two of us, with a guide, crossed the scorial ledge to the foot of the cone, where all seemed rude tiling of scoriæ over hollows. We could see the hollows, and hot breath came up from their savage mouths. We advanced in increasing heat. Our shoes were so hot that we could not keep our standing long on one place. Then, every few minutes, came a deep, muffled, and heaving sound from the bowels of the mountain, followed by a new outburst of smoke from the crater, and a new discharge of substances which were thrown up much higher than the summit of St. Paul's, and descended as a wonderful firestorm, pattering on all the slopes of the cone, some of them coming within two or three yards of us, and seemed about to fall on our heads. It was not difficult, however, to dodge them, so as to escape injury. This we did several times, to our great delight. The scene surpassed my expectation. How much to say of anything in this world !"

As I was myself present, I may add that the twilight came on soon after our ascent, and that the fiery masses thrown into the air shone out in all the red brilliancy necessary to give completeness to the picture.

CHAPTER IV.

RESIDENCE IN BATH.

BEFORE his departure for Germany, my son had become engaged to the lady to whom he was afterwards married. On his return from Italy he felt desirous that his settlement in this respect should not be long postponed. But preliminary to that step, it was expedient that he should be settled ministerially. In these circumstances, as may be imagined, he became more sober and practical than during the early part of his residence in Halle. He was still far from meaning to content himself with the usual routine of the pastor and the preacher. But what else he should do it was left to the future to determine.

Early in 1848 my son became assistant minister with

the late Rev. William Jay, in compliance with a unanimous vote of the church under the care of that eminent preacher. In many respects this connexion appeared to be one of much fitness. It seemed reasonable to expect that the aged pastor would see in the amiableness, modesty, and high sense of honour which characterized his young coadjutor, very much to deserve his affectionate confidence. It is well known that the conduct of the young preacher towards Mr. Jay was in all things as that of a son in the Gospel. Bath, moreover, seemed to be the place in which the preaching of the assistant minister—evangelical, intelligent, devout, and always pervaded by good taste—would be generally acceptable. Nor were these anticipations wholly disappointed. During a considerable interval, as the pastor had not been able to preach more than once a day, and as the assistance obtained had been irregular and only partially satisfactory, the congregation had much declined, and the future was regarded as wearing a more gloomy aspect than the present. My son's acceptance of the invitation from the church produced a change. The congregation revived; the people of Bath in general seemed at once to appreciate the character and worth of the stranger who had thus made his appearance among them.

In those days I had some knowledge of the feeling with which Alfred had given himself to the duties of the sacred office; but I did not then know much that I have come to know since. We have seen something of the wide range of culture with which his mind had been occupied; something of the ardour with which this breadth of study had been prosecuted; and something of those regions of doubt and darkness through which his spirit had been led. But from his habit of jotting down his thoughts and impressions on all subjects, we learn that the spirit in which he separated himself to his pulpit and pastoral duties was as thoughtful, as simple, and as devoted, as it could have been had he never contemplated services of any other description. Here are a few sentences written at this time, intitled, "Some considerations for securing my earnestness and confidence in my work":—

"1st. I have men's religious hours entrusted to me. Should I not strive to keep them solemn—to hold them fully attentive?—then, when I may beget thoughts in them whereby they may live, I must strive to make them *memorable hours*—must be very careful that no one may justly *wish them over*. . . .

"2d. Let me think how I may have to behold some of those perishing whom I might have saved had I been more faithful and more earnest. Let me think of those I look upon as any of them going away from the face of the Judge into outer darkness.

"3d. As the Redeemer has loved me, so must I love them. I must try to be to them His representative—having a Saviour's longing for them—hungering and thirsting after their souls—finding that my meat and drink.

"4th. Remember the great danger is that they may be the *worse* for my message—must strive all I can against this—must try so to proclaim the message that they *must love* in *believing*—must make them catch from me a deep feeling of the *verity* of these things. Let there be contagion in my divine enthusiasm. Haunted by a fear that the hour is coming in which they will wish they had never heard my voice—must strive with all my soul to save them from *that*.

"5th. If ever He helps in anything, He will help me in that. He will not refuse my prayer. He must wish that I should come to Him to plead for souls. He will help me to plead with them. He has it at heart that His representatives should strive to do His work well, and that they should succeed in it. He has given precious blood for those souls; will He deny help for them? Am I not herein obeying His very words, 'Feed my sheep'? I will—help me!"

Such was the feeling with which he entered upon his labours in Bath. Scarcely any one knew at that time how sensitive he was to every indication either of success or of apparent failure. To see that any measure of good impression had been made, even on the mind of the humblest, cheered him exceedingly; while slight and heedless things, which seemed to show that no such effect had been produced, often in the same measure depressed him. A young person is much affected by one of his sermons and comes to him for advice; and then he writes:—"This shows me that the earnest and fervent prayers I offered when I came here were not in vain; but that God heard when I called upon Him, and has sent me an answer, with more perhaps in store. I thank Him for this highest honour in the highest work. I will go on in His strength." It was this quick sensibility, and a consciousness that there was some tendency towards excess in it, which led him to say at this juncture, "How small a thing makes me sink or soar!" But there is a law in our nature which insures that the joy of success and the grief of failure shall be commensurate. We cannot have the one without liability to the other. This law, which is found everywhere, is especially present in the experience of the man who brings to the pastoral office the feeling proper to it.

He is at times almost led to wish that he had a dual nature, feeling all that he does in the circumstances of to-day, and being incapable of feeling in the different circumstances of to-morrow. But this may not be. Had Alfred possessed a more robust organization—and I should further say, had he been less modest and less humble—he would no doubt have been less affected by discouraging influences. Yet who, upon the whole, could hope to mend what he was? We must add, that while the speeches of coarse-minded men were too often allowed to disturb him, his great suffering during his early ministry came from a cause before mentioned—the fear lest his memory should not serve him effectually when in the pulpit. From all these causes, his course as a

The end, however, of my son's connexion with Bath was not such as these facts seemed to promise. He discharged the duties of assistant minister at Argyle Chapel two years. Mr. Jay had then reached the eighty-fourth year of his age. A few months after his settlement in Bath my son had married Miss Finlay, the daughter and only child of Mr. James Finlay, of Newcastle-on-Tyne. He soon had the prospect of feeling the responsibilities of the family man, and became somewhat anxious to know what his relation to the congregation was to be in the event of Mr. Jay's decease, or of his total incapacity for service. With a contingency on that point before him, Bath had ceased to be to him a place of rest. When, however, he ventured to intimate that the condition of his remaining must be his ordination as co-pastor with Mr. Jay, and as his intended successor, Mr. Jay, who, it must be owned, had always expressed himself opposed to co-pastorates, manifested hesitation. Some of the authorities, too, had their reasons for hesitancy. The pastor, indeed, at length attributed the hesitancy to the authorities, and the authorities never ceased to attribute it to the pastor. Suffice it to say, under these influences, the posture of affairs became such, that the only wise and dignified course open to my son was to resign. He did so. More than five hundred persons belonging to the church and congregation, a large majority of the whole, addressed to him a memorial earnestly entreating him to remain. Many who had not felt at liberty to sign the memorial would have been much gratified to have learnt that the wishes of the memorialists were to be complied with. But it did not accord with my son's temperament and character to remain in such a position after what had happened. The following letter was written on the 25th of March, in 1850, on the Monday after the Sunday evening on which the writer preached his last sermon in Argyle Chapel:—

"MY DEAR FATHER,

"I sit down for a few moments, in the midst of the bustle of packing, to give you an account of last night.

"It would have done your heart good to see the immense cram. The place has never been so full since Rowland Hill preached there. I was supported throughout—felt no nervousness or trepidation. The text, the two last verses of Jude.* Both aisles had double forms filled, crowds standing in the gallery and at the doors, and sitting on the backs of seats, steps, &c.

"Then, after the sermon, great numbers crowded into the vestry, to shake hands and say good-bye, nearly all in tears. At the close of the sermon many were weeping; and when, after all, I came outside the chapel, having been long detained by those who came to speak to me in the vestry, there was a crowd at the door pressing eagerly forward to have a shake of the hand as I departed.

"In fact, the deacons and Mr. Jay have no idea of the amount of interest felt in me, and the dissatisfaction at my being suffered to leave. I made no allusion in the sermon to anything unpleasant, thanked the memorialists, and all who had shown me kindness, and concluded with a solemn appeal, and good wishes for the pastor and themselves. I was encouraged by such overwhelming testimonies to my usefulness, and never felt so strongly before that I had not lived in vain.

"Your affectionate Son."

* 'Now unto Him who is able to keep you from falling, and to present you faultless before the presence of his glory with exceeding joy; to the only wise God, our Saviour, be glory and majesty, dominion and power, both now and ever.'

It may seem strange to the uninitiated that a preacher encircled by such sympathies should be a preacher saying farewell, and having a new home to seek. But the preaching of Mr. Jay, as is well known, bore the impress of a strong individuality. It had been cast in the general type of fifty years ago, and the older portion of the congregation had not only been completely moulded by it, but, as commonly happens in such cases, were disposed to take the *prestige* of their minister to themselves, and to imagine themselves great in his greatness. My son's preaching had also a character of its own, but it was of a complexion more adapted to the new generation than to the old. These facts explain nearly all that needs explanation. Mr. Jay lived to see that it would have been wise to have pursued a more generous course. Two days before his death, he requested the members of his family to express to my son his deep regret that matters had not been so ordered as to have retained his services in Bath, and begged them to assure him that he had no memory of his connexion with him as a coadjutor that was not of the most pleasant nature.

The friends of the young preacher, at a meeting convened for the purpose, presented him with a handsomely-bound copy of the "Encyclopædia Britannica." We insert his address in acknowledgment:—

MR. CHAIRMAN, AND MY DEAR FRIENDS,

It is with very mingled feelings that I now render you my heartfelt thanks for this expression of your kindness. I did not think that my parting from you would have proved so deeply painful. It has been so ordered by Almighty God in His providence that the last view I am to take of my past scene of labour here is that which presents it in its most fair and favourable aspect. It has been as though the ground had been laid out for me with the skill which is displayed in the management of some fine old gardens, where the scene widens by degrees, point after point heightens in interest, and presents some fresh element for the combination of the picture; till, at last, as the traveller is about to pass out at the gate, the full beauty lies before him—lawn and copse, grove and fountain, and meadows and purple hills beyond. Thus do I look on this portion of the ripening vineyard of God's Church, as now displayed most fully, and clad in its most powerful attraction: thus endeared and beautified by these expressions of attachment, these tokens of kindliness, at the very time when I am about to quit it.

"I can take to myself no claim of absolute freedom from sorrow, but in the step I have taken I have done nothing to create misgiving in my own mind. I see clearly the course of duty. I am firmly convinced that it is not the will of God that Bath should longer be the place of my labour in His cause—that He wishes me to go hence—whither I know not. I have done nothing hastily. There has been no precipitation about any movement in my whole procedure. I do not look back with regret on a single step that I have taken. But separation is none the less bitter from those who have manifested a feeling such as yours. Friend after friend has shown me kindness, has rendered me thanks, has overwhelmed me with regrets. The quivering lip has spoken, and the glistening eyes; and these things fill my heart with pain. God has purposes we cannot fathom at the time: sometimes He shows us their wisdom a great while after the event that has perplexed us. You have not now to learn where to look. He is with us always, even to the end of the world. We know little what God may have in store for us in some rich future. When much may look adverse, we must wait and patiently hope. Let us wait—do you wait, and earnestly pray for the outpouring of His Spirit. He will bless you, I doubt not, even as aforetime. These expressions of your kind feeling are singularly appropriate. With what pleasure will my eye rest on those volumes as I sit in my study, and how greatly will they aid me with their varied information! The selection of a gift is a delicate thing, and felt often to be fraught with difficulty. For some reasons it would seem desirable that a present should be a something elegant and ornamental—an article of taste —a graceful token of the luxury of friendship. For others, again, it is well that it should be a something often used, that frequent sight or touch may recall the giver constantly in the gift. You have most felicitously combined both these advantages in what you have given. Upon this time-piece I shall often look, and with me my beloved wife, and I shall listen to that constant sound within it which marks the passing seconds as to the beating of a heart which you have placed within it to tell of the love you bear us. The structure is of no colossal size, but it will stand up then before me as a sure fortress, a strong castle against all future despondency—the monument of the fact that I have not been suffered to labour in vain, or to spend my strength for nought. Your 'Encyclopædia,' too, I shall find of the greatest value. Such a book is among other books as the banyan-tree among other trees. A single tree may be large of girth and stately in its height, still it is but one; but from the boughs of the banyan descend the shoots, which, touching the earth, take root and become other trees—a whole city of foliage arches over many an acre, with its streets of greenery and avenues of waving shade. It is so with a great work like this—subject opens into subject, and knowledge grows and gathers about knowledge, branching over the whole domain of thought. An ingenious writer has said that if a friend should ask another to come a hundred miles to visit him, and should on their interview set before him only a basket of fine fruit (that together they might admire and converse upon the marvels of the bounty these productions represented), that the guest should think he had been rewarded to the full. You have here set before me a something higher yet—a collection of the fruit, not of inanimate nature, but of the spirits of men. Here is the harvest and vintage of the brain, and a gathering of the fruits of knowledge from every clime and every age. I fancy that your gift resembles such a display of ripe fruitage as that of which I have spoken: here are fruits with the hard shell or the prickly husk, there are the abstruse and thorny subjects in your volumes; beside them, again, are sweet and luscious fruits—the department occupied by the rich, attractive themes of sunny literature and genial art. These books will render me many a service in the days that are to come. I have never thought that divinity should be studied merely in a dry and abstract manner, as a thing by itself. To do any justice to the might and amplitude of religious truth, its thousand-fold relationships, its ever-varying application to our ever-varying life of every day, should be prominently set forth —the associations that link it with nature and with science, with the manners and opinions of mankind, with man's labour and with his recreation, with small things as well as with great, with the endeared homeliness of the fireside as well as with all that is lovely and all that is profound. It is well, therefore, for the religious teacher to have eye and ear open to all nature and all life, and to count nothing trivial or uninteresting which may lawfully interest his fellows. We should be ready to avail ourselves of those scattered and reflected rays of light which fall from every quarter on the great truths to which we have vowed our hearts. The stream that has to turn the wheel hails every alliance that will help it in its toil: it calls with a murmur to the little streams of the hills on either side 'Come and help me,' and they leap bubbling and tinkling down at the voice; and it looks up to the clouds that hang above and says 'Come and help me,' and they lend the myriad drops of their showers to swell the force of the current. It should be ever so with us in the great work on which our life bears.

"When separated finally from you, this hour, and other seasons kindred with it, will be my chosen recollection. This, your kindness, I shall never forget—all that has been gratifying in your regard I shall love to think upon, and any occurrence of a contrary description I shall endeavour to banish as completely as possible from my mind, that my remaining remembrances of Bath may be those of love, esteem, and gratitude.

"And now, may God be with you, and be merciful unto you, and bless you, and cause His face to shine upon you. Put your trust in Him. Remember that you cannot expect to prosper except as you pray for prosperity. Pray that a blessing may come to you from the labours of those who will in God's name address you. Pray that the Spirit of God would manifest Himself and dwell richly among you. Pray for this in the retirement of the chamber; pray for it at your family altars; pray for it in the house of God. We see but a short distance onward, and we must be content *not* to see. God has promised not to fail those who seek Him. Only have this assurance—He will not single you out as the first to trust in Him in vain. One word more. You have expressed yourselves indebted to me for my services among you; but be assured of this, that I have my debt of gratitude also. But for your prayers, and the encouragement your affection has from time to time afforded me, I could never have continued to labour here as I have; nor could I have enjoyed the measure of success I have been enabled to realize. There is an action and reaction in connexions such as ours. And most happy am I to believe, that in many an instance your prayers on my behalf have returned with rich blessing into your own hearts.

"My warmest thanks are yours, and my most fervent wishes for your spiritual prosperity. Though separated, we shall not, I trust, forget or be forgotten. Distance is no hindrance to our prayers, or to the swift conveyance of those blessings from on high we prize the most. We shall need again and again yet such successes as we can send each other by mutual intercession at the Throne of Grace. Of this I assure you, and promise, as in the sight of God, that you shall be remembered in my prayers, and that such blessings as fervent entreaty may secure shall not be wanting to you, if my supplications may avail on your behalf."

During the two years of my son's residence in Bath, he was chiefly occupied with attention to his pulpit services, and though no pastor, in discharging the duties of one. One of the modes in which he endeavoured to be serviceable to the young and inquiring was in writing to them. The following letter will suffice to show the fidelity and delicacy which characterized this part of his pastoral work :—

"October 16th, 1848.

"MY DEAR FRIEND,

It had been quite my intention to write to you as soon as I had thought you somewhat settled down in your new quarters, but from one cause and another, the execution of the purpose had been delayed, till meeting Mrs. S. the other evening, she expressed a wish that I should do so—a request with which I have no little pleasure in complying.

"Not that I can suppose one of a thoughtful and studious habit of mind like yourself to have been without his seasons in which the claims of our Saviour upon his heart have been seriously considered. Perhaps much of what I may say will come before you somewhat as the reflection of your own thoughts, but yet to know that you are remembered, and though distant, often thought of with great interest and an earnest desire for your soul's welfare, will not be ungrateful. How much there is in college avocations to distract and dissipate the religious feeling, I have had reason to know; but this abides true, that by God's help, devotion and study may be united; and when they are, when the devout feeling does, as it were, inform and irradiate the intellectual toil, and when the labours of the head give a fresh zest to the higher emotions of the heart, there is no sort of life more to be chosen. As you will be so closely engaged during the week, your Sabbaths

—by this alone can you be saved. Saved, on the one side, from the unhappy toil of those who go about to establish their own righteousness; and on the other, from the many sorrows of those who care not that Christ died, or that they themselves must die, but live without peace of conscience, and die without hope in God. That you may be saved from this—that no current of necessary occupation, no influence of irreligious association, may lead you so to forget Him who died for us, is the earnest prayer of

Your sincere friend,

ALFRED VAUGHAN."

The only compositions prepared by my son for the press during his residence in Bath, were the articles on Schleiermacher and Savonarola; and the materials for both those papers had been collected mainly during his student life in Halle. The paper on Savonarola is founded on considerable research, but of which no show is made. The article on Schleiermacher presented at the time, and still presents, the most intelligent and satisfactory account in our language concerning the opinions of that eminent person, and his position in relation to the history of German theology. In a letter from Bath the writer expresses his own estimate of this paper, and at the same time makes his first mention of mysticism as a subject on which he felt disposed to bestow some careful thought.

"MY DEAR FATHER,

. . . I have finished the Schleiermacher, and it is, except the punctuation, which I shall put in to-day, ready for the press. It will occupy exactly forty pages. The article would have been more complete had I put in much which I have omitted. But even then I should not have exhausted the subject, and it would have become wearisome. As it is, I do not think I have omitted to state any point of moment and characteristic of his system.

"I shall not begin to write another article at once. But I should like to fix on one to have more or less in view. There are three subjects on which I should like to write some time or other.

"1. Savonarola, for which I have much material.

"2. On Mysticism, tracing it in the East, in the Greek Church, in the German mystics of the fourteenth century, in the French mystics, and lastly in those most recent.

"3. Leo the Great, and his stirring times.

"I should like to do the Savonarola next. But I should like to know what you think on these subjects, or on any you would perhaps like better. The first and third would consist largely of interesting narrative. The second would be rather less popular, but more novel. But I find it very difficult now to read for the mere sake of reading, and I like to have something on which it may tell in the way of product.

Your affectionate Son."

This letter was written in March, 1849. The "less popular" theme of the three here named, was soon to become a favourite with the writer, partly from its being to a great extent untrodden ground in this country, and partly for some graver reasons.

CHAPTER V.

SETTLEMENT IN BIRMINGHAM.

It was soon rumoured to a distance that Mr. Vaughan was not likely to remain in Bath. Communications from several quarters were made to him with a view to his becoming a pastor elsewhere. His next home was in Birmingham. The congregation in that town which invited him to become their minister, did so with great cordiality, and the effect of time on their attachment to his person and ministry was only to make it more and more earnest and kindly. The only drawbacks upon his comfort in that position were of a nature not likely to be anticipated by the reader —viz., the largeness of the chapel, and the largeness of the town. The chapel was so large as to seem to require the presence of a congregation much too great for my son's oversight as a pastor, if not too great for his strength as a preacher, while the large town was always ready, as will be supposed, to make much greater demands upon his services than his physical strength would have sufficed to meet. But he never ceased to feel that it became him to be the student, as well as the pastor—the man of letters, as well as the preacher. The husbanding of time, however, which he found to be necessary to the combining of these two objects was often severe. His diaries show that he was wont to task himself week by week, and to review his work stage by stage, thankful for the signs of progress, or mourning over lost hours and frustrated purposes. Time often seemed to be to him a space made to be filled with only one idea, the idea we express by the term—*work*. If well occupied in that way, it was time used; if not, it was time lost. It was during his five years' residence in Birmingham that more than half the articles contributed by him to the *British Quarterly Review* were written. It was there that his chief work—*Hours with the Mystics*—was commenced, and nearly completed. It was there that he made himself familiar with the "Old German," which in comparison with modern German is almost another tongue; also with the Spanish, and even with the Dutch, adding these languages to the Italian, the French, the Latin, and the Greek in its classical and later forms, all as the sources of that direct knowledge concerning the history of mysticism to which he had pledged himself. I scarcely need say that the labour which laid up these stores of erudition was not of the fitful kind so common with men of genius, which usually admits of large intermissions. It was labour extending through years in a series, with only slight intervals of relaxation. It is true, the dryness of such studies was often relieved by excursions into the fields of general literature. Of what was passing there, he was watchful even to a greater extent than appears in his writings. The following letter to his brother-in-law, the late Rev. Peter Russell Willans, will show, in a measure, how his time was employed after his removal to Birmingham :—

"Edgbaston, 29th Oct. 1850.

"MY DEAR RUSSELL,

I seize a moment and a pen to reply to yours—to answer especially to the mental inquiries. I was, indeed, concerned to hear of poor S.'s accident; give her my love and say all that I would say if I were with you. I certainly do look forward with the utmost pleasure to some day looking in on you.

"I find the union of the two pursuits, the literary and the divine, somewhat less fraught with difficulty here than at Bath—chiefly owing to my adopted habit of early rising. A princely hour at least, if not one and a half, I get five days of the week, at all events, before breakfast, wherein no one calls, no interruption badgers me, till at last the breakfast-bell arouses me to the actual and eating world. I can endure the minor baitings of a day better when I can look back on that morning triumph over fate. More and more am I convinced that it is better to have a necessary, regular work that must be done—a *yoke*, in fact—and above all so beneficial a one as that of preaching. I find I cannot reckon very closely on so much time clear. I get thus all my before-breakfasts, and often Tuesday and Wednesday, all but the evening of one or both. Then the Thursday morning—and Friday and Saturday for my Sunday's work—and the Thursday afternoon only for the Thursday evening service. I feel I am growing—and I preach better sermons. I think of a course of evening lectures—semi-historico-evangelico-poetico-picturesque. But it will be hard to come up to the ideal.

"My dear fellow, you are right; stick to that reading for ever. Don't, for heaven's sake, be dribbled into a gossip, or compressed into a Sunday-school teacher. Let us make common cause in the pabulum way. For genuine pabulum, you must already have found out, is rare indeed. Of course the mass of our sermons must be quite popular and evangelical, but what I mean is, some broader views of truth, and meeting of scepticism, and solving of doubts, and answering of objections, in a way our evangelical pulpit has not done yet—except in the case of such men as my father.

"The manner in which Sydney Smith handles metaphysical subjects must be a fine school to study in for *popularizing* (barring the jokes), and I congratulate you on having such a book. I have found 'Guesses at Truth,' Ruskin's 'Seven Lamps,' Emerson, Longfellow, all in various ways stimulating and suggestive. Aird's 'Religious Characteristics' has some grand passages. I am about to get Guizot's 'Civilization.' Fairbairn's 'Typology'—I can recommend the 'Mosaic Dispensation' volume as having been serviceable. But above all, I find the 'Age and Christianity,' and 'Letter and Spirit,' and several papers in the *British Quarterly* to have been good starting points. Of course, as to style and manner of preaching, nothing is good but as a starting point; for if I am convinced of one thing more than another, it has been ever of the importance of being one's self: and I never had nor would have a model in my life in preaching.

"Most lovingly yours,

"VAUGHAN.

"P.S. I generally give the afternoons I can command to bits of Latin, Greek, and Italian. I hold to my old purpose of reading Tacitus bang through, and am in Ann. VI.; in Greek I read nothing but Plato; in Italian, half through Vol. I. of 'Promessi Sposi;' in German—*passim semperque.*"

The following letter will enable the reader to judge of the extent to which the writer kept up his general reading on graver subjects. It is written to a friend who was about to write a paper on Comte's philosophy, and who had solicited his thoughts on the subject:—

"December, 1853. Edgbaston.

"MY DEAR SIR,

"You have doubtless a huge subject in hand, but one to which you are well competent to do justice. I have read attentively the outline you have sent of Comte's position. I think you may find in history some strong ground against him. He masses humanity into a single developing organism—a self-evolving aggregate of intellects (forgetful of its separations and retrocessions), and then judges of the whole by himself, as though mankind looked at things with his eyes. Hence that fundamental error of supposing that all religion springs from *an attempt to explain the phenomena of the universe*—it has not succeeded in this, so to the dogs with it. On this broad principle he can be met, I think, with effect. It is such a palpable misunderstanding and overlooking of men's spiritual and moral wants, as indeed you have already pointed out.

"In Maurice's *Religions of the World* you will find some good suggestions hereon. He repeatedly urges, in the course of his brief, fragmentary, but suggestive survey, the impossibility of this position—shows that it was not a philosophical want of a *theory*, but a moral want of a *revelation*, that prompted religious systems. As to Confucius, he seems to have been a positivist, in so far as his great idea was the foundation of a certain social order, founded solely on a kind of patriarchal principle (resting on the parental relation among men), and silent altogether about the unseen world. It would be worth while to show how China, instead of following Comte's theory, provokingly contravenes it; the Chinese could not maintain even this quasi-positivist altitude, but descended—first of all, building temples to Confucius himself, and making *him* a power in the unseen world—and then Buddhism, with its idolatries and mysticisms, became everywhere popular, and Confucianism relapsed into a bureaucratic code and state apparatus. If his theory be true, the attractive power of religion should be inversely as the squares of the distance from the starting-point of humanity—the more science the less religion, the Royal Society rendering theology daily more effete, and, by a diminuendo movement, slowly absorbing it. But it is not so, and the very mistakes of men show a hunger after revelation which they cannot cease to feel by being called fools for it. No doubt metaphysics have dreadfully wasted human time, and moved round over and over again—like fishes in a glass bowl—the same eternal circle, looking, moreover, much bigger often than the natural size. But that does not help him. The metaphysical stage has not developed into the positive, but gone back into the supernatural. The Neo-Platonists are examples. Iamblichus, for instance, returning to absolute fetischism, in his prescriptions for making images of certain metals peculiarly attractive to certain deities, which deities will be constrained to enter therein and inform your statue with divine powers. So with Proclus, combining the superstitions, rites, divinations, &c., of all religions in a kind of eclectic theurgy. Any good history of philosophy will show this. Have you De Gerando?—*Histoire Comparée des Systèmes de Philo sophie*—eight vols.—four ancient, four modern—clear as crystal, judicious, fair—a good investment, I can testify.

"On Buddhism and the Persian theology, there are full and admirable remarks in Neander's first, and I think second volumes of his Church History. I think the metaphysical and supernatural stages are too inseparably connected in history to be parted off as Comte does. A cosmogony is in a large degree a personification of what are supposed *laws*. The whole system of emanation consists in intellectualizing phenomena, and rises in a *metaphysical* scale. The system of Persia, with its warring personalities of Ormuzd and Ahriman, has a purely metaphysical principle for its summit—high above both—time without bounds.

"As to a revolutionary period as the concomitant of the metaphysical stage, Comte would perhaps point to the French Revolution, and the Encyclopædists, with Rousseau, &c., and to the Pythagorean disturbances of Magna Grecia. But the supernatural element was indestructible and rampant in the French Revolution, with all its metaphysical system-building. Witness Cagliostro, and quacks innumerable, as Carlyle's history and others abundantly show. And the Pythagoreans were *conservatives*, slowly establishing themselves by a sort of aristocratic confederacy, and at last scattered—the *victims*, not the *authors*, of popular outbreak. And then, be it observed, Pythagoreanism, though unquestionably in the metaphysical stage, relapsed to the extreme of the supernatural, and sang a swan-song, dying, in Orphic hymns, and produced Orpheo-telists—the mendicant order of ancient Greece—charm-sellers, hawkers of incantations, &c. K. O. Müller's *History of Greek Literature* you will find admirable, lucid—great information in small space —but I dare say you know it. Müller points out the growth *morally* of the Greek poetry in Pindar compared with Homer, especially as regards the future state. This is not the Comtian sort of development.

"As to the military *régime* as coincident with the supernatural, as though supernaturalism were necessarily belligerent, we see both together almost everywhere, but no basis for a law like that of his hypothesis. Religion did not animate the conquests of Alexander, and the Roman legionaries were not fanatics. Religion gave a direction to, but did not create, the martial spirit of Godfrey's Crusaders and Amrou's Arabs. It was because Christianity had not really changed the rude Teutonic and Celtic races, that they fought as they did, who drank brimming healths to Christ, and rolled drunk under the table in His honour—who looked with amazement and reverence on a patience in Him, which they would have suffered death with torture rather than imitate.

"But especially see some admirable remarks on the Comtian style of studying history in Sir James Stephen's

Lectures on the History of France, where he shows that what is true therein is no new thing.

"I dare say you will find much of this scrawl incoherent; but if it lead you to some of the helpful and suggestive sources I have mentioned, you may be repaid for wading through this letter. What I have said is just what occurs to me at the first blush (blush of ignorance it ought to be), and written in much haste, under impending dining out and sermon.

"Wishing you a thriving, genial time of it, with your intellectual progeny, and a right happy new year,

"Yours very sincerely,

"ALFRED VAUGHAN.

"P.S.—Once more. Comte professes to abandon the search after *causes* and *essences*, and investigates only *laws*. But does not the discovery of laws involve, up to a certain point, the study of causes? Where are we to cease searching for causes, and why? I ask this dimly—you, from the depths of Comte, will better judge how far it applies. I dare say most of what I have said has already occurred to you, but I have put down the thoughts as they bubbled."

It will be remembered that my son's wish to write something concerning the *Mystics* was first made known to me in a letter, dated March, 1849. Many considerations disposed me to encourage him in that wish. But the subject grew rapidly under his hands. His feeling of interest in it, and his estimate of its practical value, increased with its expansion. The idea thus came, that it might be well to attempt something on the subject in the form of a treatise. It was agreed between us that this thought should be kept in view, but that in the meantime some portions of the intended treatise should appear in the *British Quarterly Review.* The article on "Madame Guyon," published in 1854, was one result of this arrangement, and an article on the "Mystics and Reformers," which appeared subsequently, was another. The intention of writing a separate work on Mysticism had now been for sometime deliberately settled. Intent, however, as my son was on writing some book which should be, from its subject, and from the labour bestowed upon it, a book of permanent value, it may be doubted, I think, whether he would have committed himself to this project had he seen from the first the extent of the field to be explored, and the difficulties in the way of bringing it under due culture. Thoroughness in what he undertook was so completely the habit of his mind, and the sense of being able to realize it was so necessary to pleasure in his work, that the enormous labour requisite to such an accomplishment of his task, had it been all foreseen, might well have deterred him from committing himself to it. Such severe and continuous effort would probably have appeared to be hardly compatible with the official duties of another kind to which he had bound himself. But every new disclosure of difficulty saw him more and more committed to his object. If at all disposed to look back, so much had been done that judgment, and even conscience, seemed to say—it is too late! So point after point was gained, until the entire literature and analysis of the theme were at his command.

A few extracts from his diary during his last two or three years in Birmingham will enable the reader to judge of the manner in which he employed his time, and also of his habitual religious feeling.

February 18th, 1853.—Well says Bulwer—courage—true courage—is patience—the fortitude which can resist—which bears up and holds on against temptation, and in spite of difficulty. True genius, instead of sighing and sonnet-writing about adverse circumstances, unfavourable position for development, does what is to be done, and works and waits. It is the false which bemoans itself and complains of destiny.

"The great thing is, that a writer should do his work, not thinking of the fame and issue mainly—save as such success is necessary to its usefulness at all—but of the work itself, and of Him to whom he does it, to diffuse certain right thoughts and right views among men, a contributor to the good influences of his time, and as helping them in blessing all time, though himself forgotten.

"Reputation—consider it, soul of mine, not as the end, but as a means of sowing right thoughts and feelings among thy fellows. Strive towards power over the thoughts of men—power that may be solemnly used as in God's sight, as being a faithful steward for His glory. Have I a brain that must be busy, a will in this direction which—with all my vacillation elsewhere—has been, and is, unconquerable? Let me pray to use it with reverent lowliness of heart, as a talent committed to me, fearing to waste or to misuse it, to allow any corner of the estate to lie waste, or any wain of its harvest to pass into the enemy's hands.

"*March 18th.*—How much to be thankful for. Health

and happiness. Conscious progress. May I diligently use, thankfully improve so many mercies!

"A good week's work. Up at half-past six every morning this week, and written, indeed, a huge quantity of the article on Madame Guyon—as good as finished the forty pages of print.

"*March 24th.*—Worked hard Monday and Tuesday, revising the Guyon; inserted some three pages of improvement in the middle. Finished it at half-past eight Tuesday night. Yesterday out all the morning. Holiday in the evening. This morning, what left of it, to classics, as I robbed that branch of Monday morning.

"*December 20th*, 1853.—A blank from various interruptions—morning lateness—loss of spirits and of interest in any kind of work. The year seeming about to close under the very same cloud under which it opened. L—— suffering (his wife) that fearful pain, and all things overshadowed by it. Alas! how little I have learnt. By this time this has recurred often enough to have taught me to bear it better. But I fear I do not—no elasticity. What would brace, however painfully, some natures, does but unman mine—so much is the feeling of the hour the master of the will. Yet let me hope that as we pray for the sanctification of sorrow, it has not come in vain. It is good surely to be put utterly out of conceit with what seems at other times so attractive, to see the vanity of nourished ambition, and how the banner on the house-top is nothing with horror at the hearth. May a Father's blessing sanctify this and all our trials, that we may together sing in an endless morn of light.

"*January 9th*, 1854.—After a visit to Manchester and safe return, L—— better than this time last year, myself better than Sunday and yesterday. Blessed night's rest. Proceed to inaugurate the work for some ensuing months amidst praises. May I be found striving towards that Christian *ideal* of what I, in my circumstances, ought to be—with a patient uncomplaining courage, bearing up against hindrances, surmounting trial, singing inward praises for many ever new mercies, husbanding time, not easily provoked, full of interest in the welfare of others, and while decided and firm in my own aims, yet entering into the condition of others, striving towards courage and a modest self-reliance and good hope, and trustful self-abandonment, labouring at this sanctification day by day—the Holy Spirit working in me mightily! So be it.

"*March 18th*, 1854 (his birthday).—Now thirty-one—Saturday evening. . . . 1. Want of methodical regular work—patient seizing of all moments and scraps. I have worked with energy at one time, not at another. This defect lies in my nature, and can only be slowly overcome. But I feel that steady, strong effort must be made, for I have to look back on acres of lost time—dandelion and thistle wastes.

"2. So many things necessary—pastoral duties, for instance, and speech-making—have here done but indifferently, with half a heart. I shall try to do all I do with my whole heart, remembering that if worth doing at all, it is worth doing well.

"3. Deficiency in steady equanimity. It might be well for all purposes with a view to correction, to keep a more minute entry here, to register rising times, lost days and parts of days, to calculate my hours more. My health is good—I take exercise—I have no excuse for idleness.

"Finally, I have met with much to encourage me. Usefulness at Bath—success of my writings—prosperous state of my church and congregation; and then, how vast a blessing, through all the year health uninterrupted, no pain. Oh! how much more I ought to have done for God with such opportunity. A year nearer to the question—What have you done with your life and its powers? And what can I say, but God be merciful to me a sinner! Let me live each day more for that day, husbanding every hour. . . .

"And now, as dusk comes on and shadows fall, I leave this page to go to my sermon. Think, then, thou who art disquieted in vain about little things of the great, and remember that these fingers will be dust under the wormy earth, and this world go on, and the concerns of thy soul with God be all in all to thee!"

Thus would he often upbraid himself as doing little, while those who best knew his habits were rather disposed to complain of his hazarding health and life by doing so much. Such, at the same time, was the grateful feeling with which he never failed to review the tokens of the Divine goodness towards him.

We publish one of his letters to a member of a bereft family, to show how he administered the consolations of religion to the sufferers in his flock :—

"Clifton, March, 1851.

"DEAR MISS E——,

It was with deep concern that I heard from your father, on Monday evening, that the stroke, so long dreaded, had at last fallen. I feel how little relief the most tender human sympathy can really bring in such a trial, and how vain it would be to urge you not to mourn. To sorrow at such a time is not to sin. In proportion to the depth of the affection cherished, must be the anguish of bereavement. The Gospel requires no Stoicism,—it offers the only consolation. I can but remind you of those truths, so full of comfort, which are already familiar to you, but which it is often most difficult to realize, when they are most needed. There hath no *strange* thing befallen you. The history of Christianity and of the world is full of such examples. Wicked men and persecutors have triumphed, the followers of Christ have been slain with the sword, —the survivors left to unpitied suffering, to penury and houselessness as well as to brokenness of heart. All these instances give tokens of an imperfect order of things. They show us that the retribution must be beyond time, and that we see only a part; that God will not suffer the condition of mankind to remain in that imperfect, and seemingly unjust, posture in which they are left at death. There will be a resurrection and a recompense. But how often, forgetting the grand compass of the Divine dispensations, have suffering believers, in their little troubled hour of life, been ready to ask: 'And does God reign in heaven, and rule these floods, and wish us well? All His waves and His billows are gone over us.' Yet have they been taught ere long, here or above, that Christ's words are still true, spoken to all His people: 'Lo, I am with you alway, even to the end of the world.' It is thus we may learn submission, as we remember that in some way, and time and world, to us unknown, this very work of death will issue in a great and good result. We see that side which is turned towards earth, the dark and sorrowing one ot this heavy cloud of trouble; but we must not forget that there is another side, that turned towards God and heaven, which is bright with glory. Beyond us lies a state in which all the emptiness of earth will be made fulness—all its deficiencies and interruptions supplied and made good—and its seeming wrongness exchanged for eternal rightness; when we shall say, 'He hath done all things well.'

"The happiness and the profit, the measure of blessing involved in the intercourse now sundered on earth, is still yours in its results, and is an indissoluble portion of your life and of yourself, and enters in the Divine purpose into your training for heaven. That good you have received from God, how great!—and yet only one among innumerable mercies; and, though so full of goodness, a lesser good by far than the gift of Christ and the Spirit's teaching, which God has not withholden from you. Shall we receive good and not evil? This, in its painfulness, is a great evil, but not so great as the good you have received has been great. The good of your love was eclipsed by higher mercies; but the evil of your bereavement is not eclipsed by darker sufferings. What might have been in the future, you know not; but I can readily believe that God in this trial may have given you the lighter of two sad alternatives, and that there is great mercy in its having come now, and not with some ingredients of bitterness more intense, which might otherwise possibly have been in store.

Your refuge is the Throne of Grace—think, at the

Cross, of One who went through the waves of a deeper water,—the sinless for us transgressors. Call to mind the wisdom and the faithfulness, so tried and true, which have led so many trusting souls, through so many ages. Add to resignation, activity. I believe that you possess the fortitude and energy needful for this. I have been happy to see you exert yourself when others would have added sorrow to sorrow by a brooding inaction. That grief will truly honour him you mourn, which shall rather open than chill the heart, and under which you will go, if sadly, yet readily and hopefully, about immediate or accustomed duty.

"My best regards to your sister, and father and mother. Mrs. Vaughan joins with me in every expression of sympathy. Committing you to the God who has provided *strong* consolation for those who have fled for refuge to the hope set before them in the Gospel,

"I remain,

"Most sincerely yours,

"ALFRED VAUGHAN."

On the whole, the years of the writer of this letter in Birmingham seem to have been his happiest years. His letters, during that interval, are many of them of a cheerful and buoyant description. We insert two addressed to his youngest sister, who was still at school.

"September, 1851. Clifton.

"MY DEAR OCTAVIA,—

I sit down to fulfil my promise of sending you a line—imagining your breakfast hour—the distribution of letters among the twenty-one—the radiant faces of some, as forsaking bread and butter they clutch a welcome epistle—and the disappointment of those who draw only a blank in the lottery of letters. . . . I said that morning I left that I had a bad cold and sore throat—was worse all the journey—went early to bed—weak as water—was laid up fairly for several days with an ulcerated sore-throat—could not venture to travel to Birmingham on Friday, and shall now not leave Clifton till Thursday next. Quite well now. J— too has recovered the Exhibition. I like to shut my eyes and realize over again its enchantments—recal the *ideal* of it, not the actual concrete, sandwiches, baskets, and top-boots of the Monday throng; but the world of glass overhead—the descending sunshine, the fountains, the trees, the gorgeousness. I don't think after all that they will make a winter garden of it, spite of the fine spectacle the artist gave us at the 'Overland Route,' as a promise of the beauties in prospect if that plan be carried out. I hope the 'soul of music' is not fled out of your 'Tara's harp,' but, on the contrary, is insinuating itself into the strings, or rather into the fingers that play upon them, and that you are successful in your attempts to waylay and collar the piano (R. would say they should be Collard's !), and get your hours of practice.

"Have been reading vol. ii. of Chalmers' Life. A fine example of what perseverance may accomplish—a lesson to us all not to give up at discouragements, but to work on and make the best of it, whether at a boarding-school, or in the large noisy school of life.

"I shall soon be setting in to hard work for the winter. I hope, however, it will not pass by without our seeing you at Edgbaston. Try and get intervals, snatches of solitude, as you can now and then, for reading small portions of your Bible, and for thinking and praying over the best things. There is no happiness without love to God. If you should ever need any direction, or wish any questions answered on these matters, be sure you do not hesitate to write and tell me, and I will give you the best counsel I can. J— sends you her best love, and Mr. and Mrs. F. will be glad to see you, should you ever be travelling this way. We have very agreeable acquaintances here. Now I shall get to work, if possible, for I write and read in the bosom of the family, while Katie plays, and laughs, and rushes about in all directions. Occasionally, of course, I long for the seclusion of my study, whither I trust ere long to arrive safely, and then to toil arduously. There is scarcely any thing pleasanter to me than hard work.

"Ever your affectionate

"BROTHER."

"February, 1852.

"MY DEAR O—

If I am to save the post, I must not write you, as you requested, a long letter. I meant to write yesterday, but was prevented. Here I am rusticating, and I am thankful to say, recovering in a great degree my usual health. I have been here a long time now, and shall be here nearly a week longer, taking exercise and trying to turn vegetable. I think I have succeeded in reducing myself to the desirable degree of insipidity which is recommended for health. I hope to go back with my brains in a properly dusty and neglected state— my thoughts all stiff in their joints for want of exercise, and my mind generally about a match for an intelligent terrier. This I do not doubt it will be satisfactory to you to know. I hear in imagination all sorts of piano and harp melodies from your quarter of London. I believe you will come home, whenever you do, quite a phenomenon. There must be a song on the occasion, with a grand *andante* movement embodying the idea of the genius of music returning to her native halls, and depositing her umbrella in the passage. As to autographs, so called because they are things people *ought* not to write, what an idea! The statue of Memnon might have scratched its head for a thousand years among the sands of Egypt without ever hitting on anything so monstrous. But I am too old a bird to be surprised at anything. There are all soits of loves for you boxed up at present, but to be opened out when we see you again—Papa, Janet, Baby, the senior Kittums (Kate), and yours to command. How I could go on; but, if I do, there will be that bell ringing post, and the disgrace—second only to the indelible dishonour of missing a train—of being too late for it. Wherefore I abide

"Your most loving
"BROTHER."

Acknowledging a present of Trench's "Proverbs":—

"Holly Bank, Birmingham.
"June, 1855.

"MY DEAR C.,

It is very odd that, though 'a fool's bolt is soon shot,' I should not have acknowledged your right welcome present ere now; but 'a rolling stone gathers no moss,' and I have been very rotatory lately, what with callers and sundry things to be despatched; but I do not mean 'to fall on my back and break my nose,' rather would I say, as far as excuses go, 'throw me into the Nile and I will come up with a fish in my mouth;' so I e'en send this excuse, though a stale fish, I confess; it is at least fact, and 'truth may be blamed, but cannot be shamed,' and you will not deny that, speaking of excuses generally, they are serviceable on occasions, and 'a friend in need is a friend indeed;' though I may acknowledge that there is much of 'lightly come, lightly go,' about them, of the 'wie gewonnen, so zerronnen,' as the Germans say—yet, 'in for a penny, in for a pound,' and, 'Le vin est versé, il faut le boire.' There is, in fact, a delicate compliment in dwelling on this theme of excuses, because it supposes you to be one of those who are not often reduced to making them; for otherwise, I should be 'carrying coals to Newcastle,' 'owls to Athens,' 'pepper to Hindostan,' or, worst of all, 'talking Arabic in the house of a Moor.' See the effect of your book—a style compounded of Sairey Gamp and Sancho Panza. I am stuffed with proverbs as a pudding with plums, or a boy with pudding; I am surrounded with proverbs, as the earth with air, as love with dreams, as an advertising van with capital letters. I am in danger of emitting them on all sorts of incongruous occasions, making my friends stare, as at frogs jumping out of a witch's mouth. I have to repress them by a powerful regurgitating movement of the muscles of the larynx. I don't find that Pulsatilla relieves me, nor are my symptoms described in Laurie's 'Domestic Homœopathy.' I must purchase the larger work; do you think I shall find my disorder among the cutaneous eruptions? How thoughtless of Trench not to see to what a state his book would reduce delicate persons. He ought to have recommended some proverbifuge in an appendix. If you know of any specific, I hope you will let me know with all speed; I am giving myself off in proverbs at an alarming rate, transpiring them, radiating them, evolving them, or what you will, and how much of me may be left before your letter can reach me, I cannot pretend to say.

"Janet is gone bird's-nesting for the family. We do not relish the idea of Hanwell. . . .

"Affectionately yours,

"ALFRED VAUGHAN."

The following letters to Sydney Dobell belong to the interval under review in this chapter:—

"Edgbaston, Feb. 7th, 1854.

"DEAR SIR,

"My best thanks for your Balder, especially for the kindly expression accompanying it towards one as yet altogether a stranger to you. In the pages of your poems I have already enjoyed an intercourse with you that makes me only more strongly desirous every time I renew it of the friendship that may be hereafter. I could not describe to you the pleasure you have given me without more of the kind of power that produced the pleasure than has fallen to my lot. It so happened that I read Balder after a period of sore mental drought, when either a multitude of minute avocations had pulverized, or a pressure of prosaic work had parched and hardened me; not one of my singing-birds had I heard for weeks, and the forlorn poets, dust-hooded, stood unregarded in their saintly niches, when behold—Balder! I entered your ivory gate, and straightway all the waterworks of Armida's garden were set playing, and a thousand pipes you opened for me spouting rainbows—that was the outset: and then, deeper and farther on, into the tragic growth of your work (suggesting so much, philosophical and religious), wherein, at last, your Titan Japetid, having been Atlas, becomes Menœtius, and after holding up the world, shoots down to such an Erebus—with what a "red right hand" outstretched over him!

"I was sorry that the second part was yet unborn, but that sense of want ought to be, or the auguries for Part II. would be less favourable. If the first part does not suffer in such division, the second must. If the first part had the completeness, not of the part, but of the poem, the second would be inevitably an appendix, but no true continuation. Most second parts, from Goethe to Bunyan, are after thoughts, and inferior to the first from that very cause—but the rudiments of yours underlie the first—the development you project is essential—at least, *some* farther issue.

"You will not be surprised at being misunderstood by

some, since you have no didactic preface—nor garrulous chorus—to act as indicator or play-bill, and disclose your plan. Hasty reading will misinterpret the purpose of the simplest prose, and much more the various progress of a poem—and now-a-days most people read as the Americans eat, at utmost bolting speed, to the grievous damage of digestion; and this not merely with that impalpable abstraction and Platonic idea called the general reader, but with many into whose hands critical responses, piping or thunderous, have been committed.

"But I hope the day will come, ere long, when I shall be able to interchange thoughts with you about many things—with the pen I do but advance towards you in leaden shoes.

"I am sorry to hear from our common friend, Mr. Paton, that the health of Mrs. Dobell is so delicate. I earnestly hope that your visit to Edinburgh may prove of permanent service to her; in this wish my wife unites with me, not without her share in my hopes concerning the future.

"I am, my dear Sir,

"Yours very sincerely,

"ALFRED VAUGHAN."

"Edgbaston, Jan. 2, 1855.

"My dear Mr. Dobell,

Work and interruptions of sundry sorts have prevented my earlier acknowledgment of a right welcome new-year's gift—welcome as from you, and likewise as itself auspicious—a second edition. I much admire the calm dignity of your preface. I often think of you, and of things I should like to talk to you about, or say when I write: but writing is such leaden-footed work compared with imagined speech, that now the time has come it produces but a note. Your poem grows on one with re-reading, a sign of genuineness and depth unquestionably, and is greatly enhanced to me by the glimpse I have had of you. Most heartily do we return your kind wishes for the young year. The Lily [his wife] is but drooping at present under a severe cold—she sends her very kind love to Mrs. Dobell. I wish the time would come when we could, as it were, take a stroll through each other's minds.

"By the way, that 'Ethel' was a great pleasure to me in my illness; had Mrs. Dobell sent us, or personally brought choicest fruits, or whatever other solacements for sickness are most welcome, I could scarcely have been more refreshed: it is full of promise—the change of character—but I am too lazy to write a critique now. Thank you, too, for 'Revelston,' so suggestive with its brief touches. When sickness is not too severe it is very pleasant to have a rhythm hovering about one's mind—circling, and humming, and soothing, as that did. Gerald Massey sent me a copy of his poems—they are full of spirit and nature—he is born lyrical. . . . As to my own affairs—my illness, our removal shortly to a new house, my disgust with the earlier portion, and consequent necessity of re-writing—and finally, the necessity of writing other things—have all combined to delay the appearance of my book—projecting it into the most uncertain future—quite as well, perhaps, all things considered.

"I abide

"Yours most truly,

"A. VAUGHAN."

"Holly Bank, Jan. 30, 1855.

"MY DEAR MR. DOBELL,

Before my bookshelves come from the painters, and I have a study, and get frozen in to hard work, and fancy it would be criminal to spend more time than could be avoided in letter-writing, I am determined at least to write to you. Motive—mainly to thank you for your share in the Sonnets (on the Crimean War), and when you see Alexander Smith pray convey ditto for his. This I like, that both he and you are ready at once to suspend whatsoever work you have in hand, and to write for the present need; that your pursuit of an æsthetic ideal has led to no Goethe-like indifferentism; that you show the world how the true poetic element is not confined to unreal legendary regions, or mere nature interpreted by crowding subjective fancies, but is to be found by genius wheresoever passion works, nobleness dares, self-sacrifice exhales heavenward. There is a manliness about this. I am sure Milton must have had his sonnets for these days, had he fallen on such degenerate ones—with, alas! no Cromwell to make Europe tremble at us. This is goodly, that men should see how genius—not querulous and egotistical, but with deepest, broadest fellow-feeling—feels more when all feel much, and has, over and above, this gift of expression to reveal and to diffuse its emotions. . . .

"So much for criticism—wherein, as the respective shares are concealed, there can be no personality, flattering or otherwise.

"We have safely crossed that wretched Rubicon—the removal from our old house into our new. I have been a stranger to hard work since my illness, and am at present without a study. Have been reading Montgomery's life, just come out, with a view to reviewing. When that task is done I may be able to set to work at the revisal of my book for the nth time (to be mathematical). I have no plan beyond, and am thankful to say, have no far-reaching plan for life at all. I try to live in the present—that present not uninfluenced by hopes and supports drawn from *beyond* time, but cleared if possible from anxieties about schemes and ambitions *in* time. If I had had the fixing of my own temporal lot (I should have made a wretched mess of it of course), I should have been a man of moderate means, able to purchase a large library, and writing histories deliberately —towards a historic ideal—doing nothing but that. I would have left some contribution to history behind me, that should live at least for three or four generations. So says the most ridiculous of follies—the notion that we could have improved our lot.

"Now see the actual. I am a preacher, conscientiously, and happy therein, liking it;—also writing over and above, as casual needs may press—and liking that; but obviously not *meant* by the Almighty to have time enough to write a great history. So placed, the wisest plan is planlessness—immediate duty—and to give up hankering after what might be well enough in quite other circumstances. As it is, though I have some of the scholarship, and all the passion, necessary for a history of some mark, the attempt, over and above my present duties, would crush me, and I can think only of fragmentary efforts. I did not mean to launch out into these confessions; but you are already a friend, and this talk carries some relief with it. I frequently feel, though I am not very aged, as though I had run the round of life—enjoyed in their turn all its best enjoyments, and as though what I could know and do, if I lived my threescore years and ten, was so insignificant, that nothing attaches me to life but my wife and children; not any hope or purpose, or mere love of living even. It seems that all I am, and all I may do or become, could be perfectly well spared by all except those of my own household.

"I hope Mrs. Dobell has found some mitigation of that protracted suffering which I can never think of without a pang—for you or for her—I scarcely know who draws deepest on my sympathy. My Lily sends her kindest love to your darling—warm and unhindered through the wastes of Arctic air that lie between us in this freezing weather. The birds welcome us to this neighbourhood, for they have rejoiced in ejected crumbs;—would that in one's most benign moods, needy and deserving objects were drawn to present themselves by an instinct as quick and sure as that which attracts the sparrows almost the moment you have shut the window. What Plato wanted for friendship is wanted quite as much for benevolence. But no more. I abide,

"Most truly yours,

"ALFRED VAUGHAN."

Letters to the Rev. Russell Williams :—

"Edgbaston, Oct. 3d. 1853.

"MY DEAR RUSSELL,

Right glad am I to hear that you have been, for some time past, making way towards the haven of health, after all your storm-tost buffettings of pain, and hope deferred, and depressing illness. You will find no small enjoyment now in quiet reading, just released from the clutches of grim torture. Butler's sermons verily deserve your praises, and I have with gusto inserted therein my proboscis. I cannot accuse myself of over work; it is impossible almost with the dissipations and pastoralities of the ministry to be an excessive time in the study. It is not with us ministers the study-work that makes the pace so killing; but every one's business, and the anxiety, and incessant Lilliputian arrow-shooting of church oversight. But I am helped in this by goodly deacons; and, moreover, have learnt to take it easy, and throw the thing off when not about it, as I could not do once; and this improves my spirits, temper, and general health altogether. A 'riled minister' is a dangerous animal.

"I write hastily, it is Monday morning, and I want before I go out to do some Thucydides. I generally take Monday morning for classics, and find that, if I did not fix on a certain day, I should never do anything at all. . . . Have been reading much of a fine German work by a man named Carriere, on the Philosophy of the times of the Reformation. The man is a vile Hegelian evidently, but worth reading nathlesse. Likewise D'Israeli's 'Curiosities of Literature' have amused me much; as also, 'Las,' a German novel in four volumes, still in hand, wherein Cagliostro effectively figures as arch-quack and comptroller-general of mysteries. . . . Katie is blooming in rude health. Be jolly and hope ever.

"Yours most affectionately,

"R. A. V."

"Edgbaston, Nov. 1, 1854.

"MY DEAR RUSSELL,

I have been wanting, for some time past, to write to you. Don't be amazed at my being so long about it; your own long silence leaves one in Egyptian darkness as to where you are; there's no extorting letters from you or S—; if you answer this, may I be a Dutchman of the first (Hollands) water! We have been to Scotland. I have come back to be ill—thoroughly ill—quite laid on the shelf now—pleurisy. I am slowly getting better, so enough of my ailments when yours call for so much more sympathy. We have both been continually inquiring after you at the College—heard of the London journey, and now lately of your resignation for six months, no doubt the best thing for you. At least you are different rather from me; I should have resigned much before. But do not regard the step as one preternaturally ill-omened, like shutting the door of ministerial life upon yourself all your days. You'll preach yet, and have a better charge than that some of these days. But I admit how hard it must be to keep up hope for so very long a time as you have suffered.

"And remember after all, my dear fellow, that success in life here is not the great object even here. Self-culture—development of all that is best and greatest in us to a quiet greatness of character—this is greater, higher, though to the jostling men of thews and sinews who were made to succeed in the ordinary sense it may look like failure. Not to preach is not to be cut off from growth and from enjoyment. To this you are called; 'this cup, shall I not drink it?'—to display, not active force constraining circumstance, but passive magnanimity in enduring with resignation where weakness would murmur—the greatness of boundless *trust* in God—it may be the other some day afterwards, but this patience which smiles amidst its tears is now your duty. Be cheered, 'thou shalt yet praise Him.'

"How is S.? Give her our warmest love. I write vilely. I am as weak as a child.

"Your affectionate brother,

"R. A. V."

In the autumn of 1854, an event happened, to which allusion is made in the preceding letter, and which threatened to increase this conflict between the claims of a pastorate and those of the press. My son consented at that time to preach to the congregation in Glasgow, so long the charge of the late Dr. Wardlaw. The Church invited him to become their pastor. It was natural that he should be gratified by such an expression of confidence, coming from such a quarter. But he saw, upon reflection, that it was in scarcely any view desirable that he should comply with the invitation. Not to mention other considerations, his physical strength, which had not been equal to his position in Birmingham, would have been far less adequate to the services that would be demanded, and very naturally demanded, from the man who should fill the vacant pastorate in Glasgow.

It was in the close of this visit to Glasgow that my son's health so far gave way as to occasion much painful apprehension. At Manchester, on his return, he suffered much from pain in the side. Before he reached Birmingham, the pain had greatly increased; and the attack proved to be pleurisy. This form of malady was soon subdued. But the patient was reduced to a state of great weakness, though care had been taken to avoid either bleeding or blistering. Two months passed before he felt equal to his official duties.

In a letter to a friend at this juncture, he writes :—

"Many thanks for your long letter. It is easy for me on the shelf to write letters, but when I was in the vortex, as you are, to write a letter of that length to any one would have been a strange work for me. I have enjoyed it, and the friendship it involves, and long all the more that you could be here, with your hopeful words and strong buoyant faith, to speak a word in season to one apt to droop now and then. I never so realised before how life hangs by a thread, or had my hold on earth so shaken, as though a weed had been loosened in its roots by a vigorous grasp and movement, though not uprooted. The possibility of my constitution degenerating rather than strengthening, and having, it may be, but a year or so, or a few years more to live, brought me to feel how much I have yet to do in acquiring perfect resignation, happy submission to any will of God, and complete escape from the fear of death. Toward these things I struggle.

"I cannot but be thankful that I have worked so

hard, and as good as written my book. The mundane element in me says, you would leave that behind at least as a trace of your existence. And it is a mercy not to have been taken away in early life, before tasting what God's goodness has made life to me. Now I have richly feasted on all this, in wife and children, and friends, and active work among my fellows. Yet do not imagine from my writing this way, that I have serious symptoms remaining. I am, to all appearance, completely recovering, have strength and appetite, voice deep and full, not a trace of pleurisy or consumption there, and so on. But, having had a narrow escape (for there was much more danger than I thought) it strikes a chill and overshadows all about you. Yet why not reason the other way, and say—spared so far, I am surely reserved for more service."

It should be added, that this more serious illness had been preceded, through years past, by frequent intervals of lassitude, and in the winter of 1851-2 by considerable indisposition. Still, as no pulmonary ailment had ever been known in the family, it did not occur to us to suspect danger in that form on any of those occasions. But on seeking further medical advice in the spring of 1855, it was found that the tendency, at least, to disease in the throat and chest, was such as to require that the patient should submit himself to restraints quite incompatible with the continuance of his office as a minister. In the summer of that year he resigned his pastorate. The people of his charge were reluctant to accept his resignation, and would have preferred waiting for a time to see the effect of rest, change, and means. But their minister could not hope that any such restoration awaited him as might consist with his continuing in a position so responsible. If he should ever become a preacher again, it must be, he felt assured, in some chapel unlike that he was relinquishing, which was large enough to accommodate some 1600 people.

CHAPTER VI.

LITERARY LIFE.

MENTION has been made of the preacher's farewell sermon at Bath. In Birmingham he was not only to say farewell to his people as their pastor, but was to retire from pulpit service of any kind for the remainder of his days. The following is his report concerning his last words to his flock:—

"June 25th, 1855.

"MY DEAR FATHER,

Last night I preached my last sermon. Though it had only been announced the previous Sunday, there was a tremendous attendance. I had the service introduced for me, and so had only the sermon and concluding prayer. I was not, therefore, so much exhausted as I had expected; and in spite of many wise shakings of the head, as to the injudiciousness of attempting anything so trying, I have I think received no mischief.

"People, generally, say I am looking better. I have now considerably increased my doses of cod-liver oil. The expressions of affection and sympathy with which I meet on all sides are highly gratifying, and especially the warm thankfulness of those to whom I have been of spiritual benefit. I think my ministry, though not of the kind calculated to fill quickly a large place, has conveyed a very large amount of instruction, lodged much right principle in the mind, and to a large class among the young been of very great service. If I have not shaken many stubborn souls, I believe I have won many wavering, and directed many anxious ones.

"So now my ministerial work is done. At least I am not to be longer distracted by two objects perhaps incompatible. The physical nature requisite for a great speaker I have never had; and as preaching, even within a subordinate measure, is now denied me, I give myself to the vocation of the pen. Thirty-five is frequently a great turning-point in the constitution. If spared and improving up to that time, I may have life enough left to do something yet.

"I have now ordered the *Examiner* again, and will send it you this week.

"Your affectionate Son."

I take the following from his diary of the same day:—

"My last sermon preached last night. I enter on a new career; whether to be long or short, bringing with it duties peculiar to itself; with trials, dangers, pleasures, altogether its own.

"I commence another period with prayer. May I more fully do, more patiently bear, the will of God in my new than in my past vocation. May I be thankful, trustful, uncomplaining, self-denying. May I remember the serious lesson taught me, that mere knowledge is indeed a vain thing without the health and spirits to use it. I could afford to part with much—indeed have parted with much I have known—it would be well exchanged, were it possible, for more vigorous health. At least, however, I trust life may be spared me to issue one sign of my existence in the shape of my book. And I am happy to know, by the signs of good I have seen, that my existence already has done much good. That the world is a little the better for my being in it."

The congregation in Birmingham presented a handsome pecuniary testimonial to their pastor on his retirement. The following notice of the event appeared in one of the local journals:—

"July, 1855.

"*The Vaughan Testimonial.*

"Amid the tumult of arms, the quarrel of parties, and the vexations of the daily contests between right and wrong, it is something refreshing to have to record the meeting held at Ebenezer Chapel, and of which our yesterday's impression contained a report. The object of that meeting was one which has our heartiest sympathy. Illness has prevented Mr. Vaughan from taking a very active part in the public questions which have stirred the town since his residence amongst us. The little he has done, however, and the few times we have met him, assured us that we had the help of a man gifted with scholarship, refined and gentlemanly in his conduct, large-hearted, and liberal in his sympathies, and endowed with a general desire to aid in every good thing, and every noble work. From this small intercourse, and the consequent respect and admiration which it excited, we can readily understand how he must have become dear to those among whom his ministerial duties have been discharged. Their recognition of his kindness towards them, and their prayer for a renewal of his health, will be shared by many outside the Church to which he belongs.

"Mr. Vaughan has not been with us very long; but

in that short time has made for himself many friends who will not soon forget him, and who will follow him from the town in his search after health with warm hopes, and generous wishes for his recovery: they will also be most happy to hear of that recovery, and upon his return to Birmingham will be prepared to give him a hearty welcome. Our town is not so rich in such men as lightly to estimate their presence, or lightly to regret their departure. We are so much the poorer by Mr. Vaughan's loss, and sincerely trust that ere long restored strength will again enrich the town by his presence and labours.

"At his beautiful leave-taking, Mr. Vaughan told his audience, 'Many of you have expressed, by letter, your regret at my parting, and acknowledged benefits received from my ministry. I shall preserve these letters. Many have told me the same. I shall treasure up those words. Many have told me the same by their looks. Those looks shall not be forgotten by me.' And now we who have not been privileged to tell him our regret, either by words, looks, or letter, do so in our own fashion; and thus beg to assure him that none will more deeply regret his absence, or its cause, and that none will more heartily rejoice in his recovery and return than ourselves."

Some verses written by the invalid a little before this crisis in his history are so expressive of his habit of looking on the relations of present and future, that I insert them in this place.

"*A Lesson for Life from Science.*

I.

Every present holds a future in it,
  Could we read its bosom secret right—
Could we see the golden clue and win it,
  Lay our hand to work with heart and might.

True it is we shall not live in story,
  But we may be waves within a tide,
Help the human flood to near the glory
  That shall shine when we have toil'd and died.

Therefore, though few praise, or help, or heed us,
  Let us work with head, or heart, or hand:
For we know the future ages need us,
  We must help our time to take its stand:—

That the after day may make beginning
  Where our present labour hath its end,
So each age by that before it winning
  To the following help in turn shall lend.

II.

Long ere foot of man the earth had trodden,
 Reigned the trees and grasses all alone,
Measureless morasses drear and sodden,
 Fern and moss to hideous height upgrown,—

Lordly races—branched and fell forgotten.
 Once the wedge-fern to his neighbours spake;
Bearded fungus, with his poison rotten,
 Grey-cupped lichen thrusting through the brake,

Fluted trees with scar-like scales that glisten'd,
 All the fingered stems of black and red
Leaned their heads, and swayed, and nodding listen'd,
 All had thought the thing the speaker said :—

'Why grow and die we here in vain, my brothers?
 Some of you graceful with your pointing spires,
Some fierce with shiny spears, and mantled others
 With ruddy hues that mate the sunset's fires;

Each with some glory—all with none to praise us,
 None we can serve, beside this creeping stream,
In this hot air whose steamy breathings raise us—
 Or can we be less useless than we seem?'

III

Ages have rolled, and shelved them down below us,
  As coal we bring them darkling up again,
Now breathing steam, they lift us, drive us, row us—
  These mouldered trees which thought they lived in vain.

Not to themselves alone they lived so lonely,
  Without a bird or beast to sing or browse;
So for another, not for this time only,
  Toil we the daytime through that God allows.

Each single struggle hath its far vibration,
  Working results that work results again;
Failure and death are no annihilation,
  Our tears absorbed will make some future rain.

Let us toil on—the work we leave behind us,
  Though incomplete, God's hand will yet embalm,
And use it someway: and the news will find us
  In Heaven above, and sweeten endless calm."

In July, 1855, my son sought a resting-place for a season at Bournemouth. The genial air of that spot, and his complete freedom from official care and labour, were exceedingly grateful to him. Writing to his brother-in-law, the Rev. P. R. Willans, he says:—

"If I had been sent into the world to become an eminent preacher, I should have had strong lungs. But I am careful to lay no plans. Hand-to-mouth living is both philosophical and scriptural could we but believe it. To be free from immediate pain and sorrow should make us break out into jubilates every half-hour—ungrateful wretches that we are.

"As to thoughts—what do you take me for? I find man to be a box-cording, bill-paying, railway-borne, brine-sniffing animal—that's my principles! Good-bye.

"Yours dreamily,

"R. A. V."

Such was his buoyant mood at that juncture. He spoke, indeed, of the pleasure he felt during some weeks, as being too great to last. And truly that feeling was not to be of long duration. Early in September, after a walk only in a slight degree beyond what was usual with him, blood came from his chest. Medical assistance was immediately obtained. The report made after examination with the stethoscope was painful. It gave no hope of cure. It spoke only of alleviation and delay. My son wrote to me as soon as he was permitted. I give the substance of his letter :—

"I have been carefully examined this morning with the stethoscope. I have asked Dr. —— to tell me the state of the case without concealment. There *is*, he says, tubercular formation. The whole of the right lung, with very partial intervals of exception, is infiltrated, more or less stopped up. He says I am better than when he first saw me, and that I have been really, and not merely apparently, improving ever since I have been here. The inflammation has been subsiding gradually, and all is now much quieter. I have recovered the effects of the rupture, but I must expect to have a return of coughing up blood. The milder air of this place, by keeping the lungs freer from irritation, has contributed to the improvement. It is also in my favour that I am no weaker, and that I have no lassitude or general depression.

"But all this is so much in favour, not of cure—he has no hope of my ever being restored to ordinary health—but of a prolongation of life. I may live some years, but always requiring the closest watching, and liable to a renewal of a serious attack on the slightest cold. He says I should not go abroad, unless I could be under medical care continually—take a doctor with me for a time. He will endeavour to diminish the evil as far as possible. . . .

"This is but gloomy news, and promises a speedier close to my career than might have been anticipated. I may still without injury write, as my strength allows—a certain measure of occupation will be good. But my *work* is nearly done—that I cannot doubt. However, I have at least been spared to complete my book, or nearly so—which may serve as an earnest of what it was in my heart to attempt. Many of greater promise have been cut off with even less performance. I hope I shall have strength given me as I need it. Love to all."

In a second letter, a few days later, he writes :—

"When the lungs are affected I fear that the general apparent good health is no security that the disease is not gaining ground. I find tranquillity in proportion as I refrain from anticipating improvement, or from fear of growing worse. I have visited too many sick beds of consumptive patients, not to know the miserable history of the way in which they and their relations cling to hope after hope—each one less probable than the last, yet as fondly embraced. 'The doctor says, if so and so can take place.' 'We are hoping much from the warm weather.' 'We think him a little stronger to-day,' and so on, till death comes and puts an end to the melancholy process. I want to escape, if I can, this wretched clinging to a life which is being drawn piecemeal away. I believe it is possible to obtain a peace which shall be in a good measure above earthly hope and fear—shall tremble no more at a bad symptom, and exult no more at a good one—but shall live in this present hour and in heavenly hope, overleaping the interval between. This I mean to seek, am seeking, and hope to find. In the present I have every comfort, no pain, the tenderest and most assiduous nursing, the means of procuring whatever I really need, and so cause only for thankfulness. If I can only overcome the trial by ceasing to see it as such, and rise above all fear of death, swallowing up that fear in a more heavenly hope, I have nothing more to wish for. . . .

"Many thanks for your sympathy and counsel, and kind offer. I trust I am enabled truly to follow your advice—ready for the worst, hoping the best. Surely, after a life of so many mercies, it would be sinful for me to complain of its abridgment sooner than I expected. And what multitudes at this very time are cut off in the prime of early life amidst the horror of war!"

The day when this medical report first reached me was the darkest day in my history. This stroke came not on the branch only, it seemed to descend to the centre of the root. I felt that the severance threatened left my very nature poor. It was not so much an outward object as myself, my better self, which seemed to be passing away from me. Hopes cherished through half a life fell like a faded flower. Untruthfulness seemed to have come into the memories of the past. The visions of the future vanished. The void produced a heart-sickness such as men do not put into words. But the son did not charge God foolishly, and I trust the father did not. We had both been made to know in whom we had believed.*

In a week or two the effects of the illness at Bournemouth seemed to pass away. My son then removed to the neighbourhood of London. The advice obtained in the metropolis, though confirming the previous report as to existing disease, gave him hope,

* Writing to an esteemed friend at this juncture, he says:—"I am able to do a little at writing, but I try to sit loosely to everything, and to reach that *sainte indifférence* which my mystics counsel. I am rather tired of trying to know, and knowing so little after all; the passion for knowledge is strangely quenched within me—it seems no use, and as fact recedes imagination brightens. I have never laid long plans, and so now I have none broken; and I was always impatient to do what I had to do *to-day*—a wise impetuosity as it turns out."

not only of alleviation, but of probable cure. It was natural that both himself and his friends should be disposed to welcome this view of his case, and in some degree to confide in it. The treatment which was then commenced was extended through the next two years. The patient was scrupulously observant of all the means prescribed for him. At times the unfavourable symptoms seemed greatly to subside, and the hopeful view concerning the future seemed to be greatly sustained. But these brighter intervals were followed by others of a different complexion. Still, during the greater part of this space of time, the hopeful seemed to preponderate, and the invalid showed himself capable of a considerable amount of literary effort.

The printing of the *Hours with the Mystics* began in August, 1855, but was not completed before February, 1856. In that interval many of the later portions of the work were carefully revised, some parts being abridged, others expanded. The work soon obtained the kind of recognition from the press, and from the public generally, to which it was entitled. Deep and fervent was the gratitude of the author to that Providence which had allowed him thus far to mature the fruit of so much labour.

During the first six months after leaving Bournemouth my son resided in St. John's Wood. The next six months he passed with friends in different places. He then engaged a house in Alexander-street, Westbourne Park, London, which was his home until October 1857.

Of his mental history during these last two years of his life, the best evidence is furnished in his writings which belong to this period, in his letters, and in entries made in his diary. The articles contributed by him to the *British Quarterly Review* during this interval were on Lewes' "Life of Goethe;" "The German Courts;" "Piedmont and Italy;" "John Tauler and Middle-Age Mysticism;" and on the "French Romances of the Thirteenth Century." To these may be added a paper in *Frazer's Magazine* on "Art and History," and many shortei papers and criticisms. The following extracts are from his diary:—

"*December 23rd*, 1855.—Christmas time—Sunday evening. Here I take the opportunity of recording the great goodness I have received. To be so well as I am in circumstances so critical—the affection and the sympathy about me—the possibility of our united enjoyment of this season. Pursued, too, by the still unquenched affection of friends left behind at Birmingham, as though to remind me that the bygone preaching and old work have not been in vain.

"I call to mind His coming to our earth, entering on this life, and living through life—our life for us—up to about my very age. With us always, to make the victory ours. May I follow His self-devotion. May He raise me above fear of pain and dying, conquering me, and help me now to yield myself up freely and cheerfully as He bore His cross, to whatever is the Divine will. Oh! perfect in me Thy 'Not as I will but as thou wilt.' Who am I that I should expect all to go well with me and have nothing adverse? I must work the works of Him that sent me while it is day; the night cometh when no man can work. If our work is that of Him that sent us and not our own, we shall be continually committing it to Him, and not be dwelling on its possible after benefits or ultimate issues. We should do it as those who have but *one day*, and know they must in a few years lay by their tools. Blessed be He who made His life *human* to make ours *divine*.

"*December* 30*th*.—Sunday—last of the year. How important to remember that while we are writing our lives in act on the growing page of the past, God is recording our biography—has His lovings and His judgments, His praise and blame—an hourly secret judgment always going on.

"Also that God having set us in a certain position, endowed in a certain way, has His idea *of* us and *for* us; that we should try and ascertain what that is—what is our Father's work—our place and purpose in the world between the eternities—the building and the builded.

"*March*, 1856.—Yesterday evening at A. and M.'s. Slept there—home this morning. Great enjoyment. What shall I render? Open wider the door and let blessings more amply in—yea, let Christ the Blessed and Perfect in. So shalt thou express thy thanks. To do this thou must meditate thankfully on thy many blessings, throw off faithless anxieties and fears, forget self, and in this way, while seeking to acknowledge what thou hast received, thou receivest more, and art growing in larger capacity for blessedness. Clear space for happiness.

"*Heart's Syllogism.*—We live and move and have our being in God. But God is love. So we live and move and have our being in love.

"*Brotherly kindness.*—'Inasmuch as ye did it unto the least of these.' The members of a household, the friends with whom you correspond, all your Christian circle, are these members of Christ to serve and make them happier, to rejoice and comfort them, to save them pain, and give them joy, by love, by cheerfulness, by self-sacrifice. This is to serve Christ. Let thy thanksgiving run out into this—let a fellow-creature, a brother, be happier. Amen. I can make no return to Christ, but I can gratify Him by loving and aiding His own.

"*April 28th.*—At Cliffe. Have been here about four weeks. A season of blessed rest—walks—loungings—quiet, &c. Read Felice's *French Protestants; Life of Grotius*, by Butler; parts of Beaumarchais and Alison; the *Yellow Frigate*, *John Halifax*. Have enjoyed a goodly cessation from production, till now I almost wish to be at it again.

"The more I read of the doom of wrong into which some of the most excellent have been born, the more am I persuaded that what we have to aim at is, not to accomplish any certain thing, to do any certain good, but in whatever position we are placed to make it minister to heavenly-mindedness—to spiritual conformity—this is hearing the Shepherd's voice; so may an abbreviated, maimed, and persecuted life still fulfil itself in bearing, in witnessing, which may be enough for this existence—the rest above. So to be contented, grateful—enjoyment in prosperity, patient in tribulation, making all a help to faith, and a means of drawing God-ward, instant in prayer, warm and broad in love, vigilant and strenuous in working, if work be possible, this is to live. So the life will be woven for us by God (suggested by reading Felice).

"The fewer mere *wishes*, generally the more *willings*, and to will rather than to wish, is the difference between strength and weakness.

"So to mistake *difficulties* for *impossibilities* is the error of the weak. Here lies the difference between those who do *something* and those who do *nothing*.

"Most lives are insignificant, not from want of *ability*, so much as from want of *exertion*.

"*May* 15*th*.—'First last and last first.' Self-seeking forbidden—ambition—mere desire of eminence for eminence sake—the desire of the name as much as the thing—the excess of elation or depression at praise or blame—exacting love of being first in affection, or demanding affection more than is natural, inconsiderately, with calculating jealously, not radiating love, but bargaining for it as a return. All these are forms of self. Let them be accounted as so many sources of danger and disquiet, as enervating character, above all as littleness inconsistent with the 'High Vocation.'

"Let me seek to come up to my *own standard*—to what God has given—to do my best, and leave reputation and success with God. How evidently is this *use* of talent—this faithful diligence, the main thing with Him who appoints as He will the mere adjunct of applause from man, but looks to the heart Himself. Let me pursue with this faithful calmness each growing and successive ideal as duty after duty arises, regarding myself as answerable only to God, and so living above, not only envy, but ambition too. Beloved Fénélon has perhaps more insight here than I once thought.

"I am striving towards an historic style—a narrative that shall mark great phases with a kind of philosophic comprehensiveness, with a selection of vivid detail, grouped chiefly about the great men and real action of the drama—a biographic-representative summary of main features, if possible giving the generalizations in some illustrative or emblematic form, dwelling on individual conflicts, hopes, fears, on dramatic situations poetically coloured. Remembering as minor rules:—

"1. To demand as little as possible of the reader.

"2. To avoid the abstract and seek the concrete.

"3. To characterize by some epithet, when possible, names and places, that they may convey some image to the reader.

"4. To aid memory by antithesis and point—repeating foregoing words.

"5. Having no sentence too full of ideas. To detain the reader over an idea or illustration, giving it in a succession of sentences, each complete rather than in an involved metaphor, or half-metaphor half-simile.

"*July 20th*, 1856.—Birmingham, Sunday. This morning at chapel once more! I look back on the year since I left—it was just about this time last year when I left this neighbourhood, having preached my last sermon June 24th, 1855.

"I call to mind the first glad fallacious weeks at Bournemouth—the writing in the mornings—the sands—then the dark illness-time—and the voice which said so tenderly, *Ye believe in God, believe also in me.* Then the London journey on the misty autumn morning. . . . Seeing this morning the old faces within the old walls, meeting the hands grasping mine, the glad or tearful eyes, the blessing of God in His house, the presence of Christ visible by faith—all these things make me feel hopeful, peaceful, and vigorous. In all these things God is revealing Himself to me as the one unchanging good amidst all changes—my stay and hope—what fulness of mercy—how far better than my fears. Blessed be His name. . . . What goodness to my darling—to my little ones, sparing and blessing them to and for me, keeping us thus loving, happy, blessed. Oh, my God, how manifold are thy mercies! Open thou my lips, and my tongue shall show forth thy praise. Draw me nearer to Thyself, and keep me there. How precious the *humanity* of Christ. How near that seems to bring Him, and He took the burden, and bore the pains of life, that we might have its enjoyment. What tender mercy to live in as an atmosphere—the ceaseless nearness of our Lord. Oh for more of His spirit, less of self, more thought for Him—His service—His pleasure. Show it me, oh divine Master, every day.

"Evening. A truly happy Sunday this! Full of mercies. I ask for wisdom to endeavour to survey my position, to see it as from its true view in God's sight; as to me in a spirit-state, looking down on the earth. It is a place in Christ's kingdom. That kingdom consists in spiritual truth, also in all goodness, all maintaining of truth against falsehood, all that makes men more true, loving, happy, all that contributes to their true well-being, is part of that kingdom. I with my pen am appointed, as by the hand of my Master, to the work of conscientiously advocating and diffusing truth, knowledge, love, against error, ignorance, hate, and misery. God give me patience for the conscientious discharging of this service. May I be a faithful steward, and render my Master His own with increase. God illumine, elevate, invigorate this brain and heart—these thoughts and passions, sanctifying all my nature, giving more and more.

"*August 3rd.*—Sunday afternoon. The other night, lying awake, I reviewed the last ten years of my life. What goodness and mercy! The common lament of lost time, of aimlessness, is not mine. There has been no lack of energy in that work to which I set my hand, nor any looking back; but my remissness has been in not living more near to God—defective spirituality. . . . I wish to set my affections more on things above. I seem to have lived a very long time, and now feel as though I had no particular work to do. Had I health I should be as ambitious as ever; but the uncertainty of life extinguishes such plans. I am in a sense necessary to my own dear ones, otherwise there is little I can do now. I should not find it easy to think of leaving them. But, setting that aside, what are a few more years of this life? To have dying well *over—behind* me not *before*, and life's trial ended happily, would be bliss indeed. But let me not doubt the Son of God. Is death worse in real danger than thirty years of life? Surely not. Have I not been marvellously *kept?* Then I can launch out, I hope, trustfully. Oh, forsake not the work of thine own hands. At least let me live as if living only for each single day as God gives it. My lot at this moment abounds in mercy. Hear my cry, oh Lord, may I be ready when thou comest. This is my duty—the plain duty of my position, not to be afraid. I cannot proclaim Christ, cannot actively serve Him, but I am bound to glorify Him by rising above the fear of death. Is not cowardice treason? Fear not then death, saith my Lord. Great words—the power of death is broken! Captivity is captive. May Christ set me free from that disgraceful bondage—fear of death. Thy will be done.

"*January 1st*, 1857.— . . . . O Lux mundi! da mihi

lucem! Multa in uno precor—da mihi sapientiam. Grant me this year with more of self-forgetful wise-heartedness to fulfil my duties towards those about me—to repair some of my numerous hiatus valde deflendi—to rise to a higher character—to reach a better point to start from at death for the eternal progress of thy world above. More calmness, patience, capacity of suffering—how? by more of Thee! and by diligent *action*.

March 18th, 1857.—(His last birthday.) Now thirty-four years old. How mercifully spared! Christ is Providence to me—the hand pierced gives me this continuance of life. My *Life* gives it me. He will animate it—He will, as I pray, make me bring forth more fruit, true Vine that He is! For this He died—for this very purpose, that, whether we wake or sleep, we should live together with Him. How precious is that humanity to me. How it enables me to realize Him—the wondrous, far beyond and above, yet mine, and every thirsting needy soul's. Unimaginable, inconceivable love and wisdom!

It should be stated, that in these diaries there are entries which show that they were not expected to pass into other hands—that the object of the writer was simply to become by this means more deliberately observant of his own mental habits, with a view to self-improvement. It will be seen that the character presented in these private records, and in his letters to his friends, is the same, and all who had personal intercourse with him will be prepared to say, that the information derived from these sources conveys but a very inadequate impression of the charm and worth of the writer.

To the Rev. P. Russell Willans, of Halifax, nearly two years after his visit to Bournemouth, he writes as follows:—

"Queen's Road, St. John's Wood.
"March 22, 1856.

"My dear Russell,

"Not that I have anything to say, but I take a fancy this morning for saying 'how d'ye do' to you, my dear fellow. My blessing on the remedies that amend you. May you improve in rapid ratio. I am still keeping better, and beginning to enjoy spring. I am miscellaneous in work, desultory, dabbling. Herodotus and Diogenes Laertius are my skimming pools in Greek. The latter is a wonderful gossip—almost a sort of Greek Burton, for the abundance of his quotations, and anecdotes, and says so-and-so's. What I want to dip into next is Cudworth, with Mosheim's notes. Are not you inclined quite to agree with him that Theism must have preceded Polytheism among all heathen nations, in opposition to Hume and Comte; and that the consolidation of deities into a unity, which is so manifestly taking place in the theology of Herodotus, is in reality a return to an old forgotten view, not the introduction of a new one? Tacitus still delights me, but I think the thirteenth Annal more corrupt in text than any other book of his, and abounding in passages so enigmatical, that Ruperti is a *Deus ex machina*, really. Do not some of Macaulay's summaries of argument, on either side, remind you of the best speeches in Livy and Tacitus? I admire them extremely, though I believe wretched critics peck thereat. What do you think of the theory of a French psychologist and scholar who will have it that the dæmon of Socrates was his *monomaniâ*, and, that on that point, the old gentleman had a screw loose? By the way, I thought Socrates said the dæmon who only told him *not* to do this or that—was, as we thought, conscience.

"If ever you can come across a volume published by Talboys, of Oxford, some years ago—'Heeren's Historical Essays,' you will enjoy it. There is one on the. 'Political consequences of the Reformation,' masterly: and another on the 'Rise and Progress of the Continental Interests of Great Britain;' the latter

I have not yet finished—it is admirable. Have you seen Weiss's book on the French Protestants? If so, send me word how you like it. We expect to leave here in about a fortnight, and go into Kent for two or three weeks. Then we purpose going to Clifton to visit; thence to Birmingham, if all be well.

"Embrace S. for me. Give my loving remembrances to all at Park Place, and

"Believe me, abidingly,

"Your brother,

"R. A. V.

"You will see an article on Goethe, by me, in the next British Quarterly."

"Clifton. May 28, 1856.

"My dear Rus.,

"How are ye? Send us a line. We have been rusticating in Kent. Now have been here three weeks, with the children in whooping-cough. I am keeping in an encouraging state, though still, I need hardly say, rigidly careful. I hope you are making way, however slowly, towards final restoration. Cheer up, my dear fellow; we shall know more about these things one day, and praise God for every trial. Never did I suspect that we should, either of us, be thus laid aside from preaching. I only thought of our doing our best therein; but I am sure there is just as much love to us in taking us out of the pulpit as there could have been in sustaining us in it. I do not take the number of souls a man converts as the certain criterion of his real position in Christ's household. To improve to our best what is *given*—whether a narrow seclusion or a 'large room'—that is the great thing.

"Need I say how uncertain my future is? Let me be like Luther's bird that sings on the bough and lets God think for him! I think a pupil or two, till something else presents, the most likely thing.

"Have been, while here, writing on the German Courts. I have Herodotus, and Carey's Translation, but no Lexicon. My plan is to open the book at random, take a chapter, translate it as carefully as I possibly can without any help; then look at the translation, and see what the words are I did not know, and what my mistakes have been. It is like a piece in an Examination Paper one has not seen before. I find that it impresses the words and idioms infinitely more than if one looked out in a Lexicon in the ordinary way. It cultivates the divining instinct, too, and disciplines you well in the significance of middle voice, and the meanings of cases after prepositions. Am also reading at intervals Hannibal's Campaign in Livy, from crossing the Alps.

"Give our love to S., and remember me to all

my dear old friends at Park Place, if you are with them.

"Your loving brother,

"R. A. V."

From a letter to the same:—

"Harbourne, Birmingham. Sep. 2, 1856.

"Me dear Rustle,

"Faith an' if it's a letter I've lately resaved of your's, it's neither here nor there, that I know of, and it's miscarrying that it's been after bein', I'm thinkin'—for divil a bit did I seed on it; and so o hone, but it's your honour's words have been lyin' in post-bags, or mayhap, leastways, anyhow, got trodden under foot of railways, or other horned cattle, bad luck to them, bedad; and yer precious langwige gone to the bad, and niver come to no good—that is to me your persayne, but belike, crumpled and rotted in the circumpendibus of a postman's breeches, or the crack of a post-office floor; or mayhap dropt by the sarvint as tuk it to the post, when she was kissed by the muffinman comin' quick round a corner, or dropt, or blowed, mayhap, in a high wind into a field, and ate by a cow, and convarted into milk, bein' white all ready, and your words may have been drunk (which far be it from me to call your honour that I should say so) by a humble family at their brekfusses; or evans knows wot besideses mightn't have cum to that ere blessed letter that's now strumfished in the bag of oblivion, or wanderin' in invisible smithereens of atoms, or whiffs of gas, through the airs and grasses (graces ?) of this vassal globe. . . ."

Such an indulgence in humorous nonsense was not uncommon with the writer, especially when writing to persons whom he knew to be disposed towards the same vein. The following letter is to a friend :—

"7, Queen's Road, St. John's Wood.
"October 20, 1855.

"MY DEAR R—,

"Greatly did I rejoice in your visit (I only wish you could repeat it often), and I write the sooner to say how much pleasure you gave me—your health and energy benignly contrasting with my weakness, and surrounding me with a bracing atmosphere. Your Paris trip must have been the most sublimated quintessence of sight-seeing, and I hope the fag of the fag-end thereof has long since evaporated. A happy thought that of yours about the magic lantern—fain would I hear your comments, and see the physiognomies hearkening. I have not been quite so well since you left, but am now again improving. I trust Mrs. H. is better, and M. and the chicks well. I cannot say that I am yet doing much work. I hope to get strength by degrees. Dr. R. says I go on well.

"What you mentioned in one of your letters to me should be an encouragement to you—it is not the *bulk*, after all, that tells—nor is it of time, or words, or even of mere thinking—it is the intensity of brief seasons; they may be threaded or not—the little read well, pondered, and germinating.

"To live much alone in spirit is seldom promotive of gladsomeness; but, though often sad, mostly safe—for he who is much alone cannot afford to despise his conscience. That landlord of the House of Solitude will make it too hot for any tenant who tricks or beards him. But I prose.

"With kindest regards, wherein my wife unites, to your circle.

"Believe me, yours most sincerely,

"ALFRED VAUGHAN."

"7, Queen's Road, St. John's Wood.

"March 5th, 1856.

"MY DEAR MR. DOBELL,

"Having at last, after so many hindrances and interruptions, been enabled to complete my book, I find it one of the pleasures of such a time (and not the least) that I can send you herewith a copy thereof.*

* *Hours with the Mystics.*

"I remember your once saying that you did not think I should always remain a minister. I little thought how your surmise would be fulfilled ere long by an illness incapacitating me for preaching, and rendering my future most uncertain. But it is much that my health is so far in the way of restoration that I can hope yet to be spared at all. And as to the rest, I have experienced such an over measure of goodness in my life hitherto, that I cannot say I feel any serious concern about my subsistence or occupation in the future. I had an offer made me after my own heart some little while ago—the Professorship of History at the College of the Presidency in Calcutta; but the probability of advantage from the climate of India was not strong enough to induce us to sacrifice England. My having weathered the winter seems to justify my determination.

"I should have written to you long before this, had I not been so closely engaged in re-writing, correcting, &c. &c. We have been very sorry to hear that Mrs. Dobell has been again so much worse. We so often think and speak of you both. I trust better days may be in store; you must both have been, indeed, severely tried. It is a grievous thing to see the heaviest sufferings alight when they seem to be least needed; indeed, but for the fact that the Most Holy suffered most intensely, it would be insupportable.

"How much do I wish I could see you! but of that

there is little prospect. Let my book supply the place of voice, as yours has so often done to me. You will know me more fully after reading it; for, though no work of art, yet my life, for some years, has been wrought into it, I scarcely know how. I shall be glad to hear from you, at your leisure, where you think the strength or weakness lies, what you consider faulty on æsthetic grounds, or where you differ from me in the judgments I have formed. We have been touched and delighted by your 'Kintra Wife's sang.' I am glad to hear that you have more such shafts in your quiver. To produce them at intervals will relieve your mind under the weight of your larger work, and, if published, they will, I think, be sure to help it. Occasional poetry of the more objective kind wins readier recognition, and serves to exhibit that healthy breadth of sympathy which prejudice often denies to a subjective work of art. We have made the acquaintance of Miss James and Miss Mulock, and see them pretty frequently. We like them very much, and feel indebted to Mrs. Dobell for so pleasant an addition to our circle here. My Lily desires to send to your sufferer the kindest expressions of sympathy, and believe me, ever in truest regard,

"Yours,

"ALFRED VAUGHAN."

To a friend :—

"7, Queen's Road, St. John's Wood,
(Early in 1856.)

"My dear R.,

"This is my first holiday-week, hitherto I have been so busy with the book as to have neglected almost everything for it. A good sign, you will say, if I am able to work at that rate. So it is, I am thankful to have to tell you. With a few temporary drawbacks and fluctuations, I have gone on well, though what may be called recovery (supposing it eventually to take place) cannot, under the most favourable circumstances, be realized in less than six months. But, meanwhile, I have no pain, little cough, good sleep and appetite, and can work to purpose, if I do not do too much at a time. The cavity still lessens as the consequence of inhaling. . . .

"I am glad to hear that you tried your project. And do not be badgered inwardly by too refined a sense of imperfection. Life is too short for that. All our efforts are such mere approximations. If the drawbacks you perceive were removed, you would see others, as through a glass of a higher power, and your ideal, like that of all truly reflective minds, will perpetually distance your actual. But, it is *under such conditions*, as imperfect creatures, that we have to work, and, while ever pressing forward, we know we can never attain. We are greatly the better for attempts in which we can pick holes innumerable. The men who have benefited the world much, have striven and wrought with such tools as they had, and have not been too nice in speculation. We cannot cut faggots with a razor. And, as to others, benefactors have often to serve men in spite of themselves—most often so, says all history, and the great thing is our own judgment of ourselves after all. Anything better than letting any quality given us be unused. We are not answerable for gifts, nor for results, but for the manful effort to use for God whatsoever He has given. We never long keep what we do not use, and use does in reality multiply gifts. Therefore do not gratify the Devil by any sign of weariness in any sort of well-doing.

"I will let you know when the book is born—sometime this month, probably. If I am well enough to visit Birmingham in the summer, I may run over and see you after all.

"I am sorry to hear no encouraging account of poor dear Tom, through L—. He can scarcely be fit to encounter the anxiety attendant on an attempt to break into the literary arena.

"Our joint love to M. and bless the children! My wife is well, and bairns, thank Heaven!

"Most truly yours,

"VAUGHAN."

(1855 or 1856.)

"MY DEAR R.

". . . . . In thought and meditation my interests are countless, and I touch a thousand points—but when I have to quit the study for a tumult of voices—to bear with and to win the humours of men—I have only a sense of duty to support me, not the sense of conscious dexterity—the case with the man who really enjoys the excitement of such collision. I am less patient in actual speech with what seem to me weaknesses, affectations, crotchets, obstinacies, than I suppose all sober-thinking souls are upon reflection; yet I believe there are those with whom meditation aggravates and makes to rankle any supposed opposition, malignity, or slight. I have little love of argument for its own sake, and am for the most part more roused to dispute with my friends than with indifferent persons or mere acquaintances. If I think I see a friend with a wrong opinion I must endeavour to convince him. But if the person be not a friend I am very often too indifferent to what he may think to take the trouble or incur the unpleasantness of trying to set him right. Why should I bother myself—says my phlegmatic habit. The moment I suspect any one is arguing for argument's sake—or not giving me his real opinion, but taking up the opposite ground just because it *is* the opposite, that moment I stop—converse on the weather, &c. It seems useless, utterly, to discuss for anything but truth, use, or good of some sort. The badinage of humour—of fancy—of mere riotous animalism, is congenial to me; but the badinage of *logic*—*i. e.* sophistry—intolerable. Is it true that you expect more from men and human effort than I do, and are not satisfied to see such an unconscionable lot of tares—not satisfied, but in a sort reconciled as inevitable? Are you not more sanguine—more hopeful of men—less inclined to let present things take their course? Has not the unknowable and the unnameable more power to make you restless? You may be surprised at all this wandering egotism, but I have been thinking, or was some nights ago, when lying awake, over your character and mine, their points of similarity and difference. We cannot combine impossible advantages. Each has some over the other, perhaps. I think some one combined of us two would be worth making. I think we were very like each other in original disposition—then different from different external conditions—but are now approaching each other again—each becoming a compound of the past circumstance and the native disposition—growing in mutual likeness.

"Give our love to Mr. and Mrs. H. I hope the boy amends, poor dear little fellow.

"Abidingly yours,

"VAUGHAN."

To the same :—

"7, Queen's Road, St. John's Wood,
"Spring, 1856.

"MY DEAR R.

"Not that I have anything in the world to say—but, as it were, to recall the savour of your pleasant visit the other day, I drop a line of How d'ye do. *Pour moi*, I still improve, thank Heaven! How goeth it with you and your household? I have been miscellaneous since the completion of the book, dodging among corners of antiquity, and re-animating the past to my mind in irregular spots; now sympathizing with Greece, exposed to the 'imminent deadly' Persian—now with Rome, as the last shadowy forms of the commonwealth vanish under Nero—now with betossed and becursed heretics of the Middle Ages—and now with Germany, oppressed by the bitterness of corrupted Lutheranism in the days of the odious *Formula Concordiæ*. Such are my pleasures; give me my wife and children, and I swear I was made for a cloister, or at least, some quiet cathedral, close, ivied, and echoing to the caw of ancestral rooks, where musty volumes and stained glass windows invite to studious thought, and exclude the noisy present. But I shall not, I know, succeed bread-and-cheesically, if I indulge such tastes. By the way, as you have the 'Life of St. Theresa,' you can judge for yourself concerning my estimate of her. Am I too hard? Is there too much satire in the description? If you think so, say so —and *why*. I should like to see how it strikes another mind. Mind you, I regard my book after all my pains, only as an *approximation* to the truth, and am ready to re-consider my judgments on receipt of fresh facts or more light. The book is selling well. I wish you would take in the *British Quarterly Review!* It wouldn't ruin you, and you would help a manly and liberal undertaking which has done much to raise Dissent above its natural faults.

"Our united best remembrances to Emily.

"Yours right truly,

"ALFRED VAUGHAN."

To the same :—

"19, Alexander Street, Westbourne Park,
"Nov. 1, 1856.

"MY DEAR R.

"I was exceeding glad to behold your handwriting once more. So you have been working away, and fulfilling the time-honoured law of toil. I don't know whether it is not pleasanter and best to get off into quite other times in the winged car of books, than to throw one's self into the present to be vexed by the dislocation of all things. The world won't wag to one's mind, wrong is so masterful : unless you can look dramatically on the nations as groups of figures appearing on a stage and playing parts before you. It is true that every man walketh in a vain show—then is it not the truth to regard the world as such a puppet-show—of a truly sublime and tragic sort—but still a spectacle? Then your idealism is the reality, and the so-called reality to you a phantom.

"I have been much worse of late—that is, *was* so some two or three weeks back—am now mending again, but have much ground to fetch up. I have had frequent intervals of total want of interest in things mundane; and as it is, my tenure on the earth seems so fragile, that I do not set hand to anything very heartily. The worry and fatigue of getting into our house here threw me back. You must have had much anxiety about Robbie. Our chicks have both been well—the sickness visiting the senior branches in our case. Some trouble must come somewhere. . . . . I am glad Derby Road flourisheth once more. I imagine you and M. among the stripped trees and autumn leaves—the quiet of Broadgate and the old turns of the Nottingham Road, once so familiar to me, and I feel how time glides by, and the knowledge of the great mystery of the other life comes nearer and nearer. May we find our best hopes surpassed!

"My wife sends love to M.—whereto add mine, and

remember me to your Nottingham circle, failing not, when next you write, to send word to Mr. and Mrs. H. and T. and L.

"Your loving friend,

"R. A. VAUGHAN."

To the same :—

"19, Alexander Street.

"November 24, 1856.

"MY DEAR R.

"Many thanks for your long, kind, and very welcome letter. I know what a busy man you are, and do, therefore, the more appreciate so liberal a measure of friendly talk. Singularly enough, only a few days before your letter came, I had been seriously meditating writing some occasional and miscellaneous fragments of a more devotional character which might some day make a little book. I sometimes ask myself whether I may not be able to do a little good that way, now that I am not to preach. How happy should I be, if I could still be of use to the Church of Christ, and obey the injunction, 'Feed my sheep.' I might thus occasionally employ myself without at all endangering my health—nay, with positive advantage thereto—since nothing would raise my spirits so much as the thought that I am still engaged in some work which our Master had for me to do. I have on Sunday evenings, when at home, dictated a little that way to my wife, and may continue to do so, unless, as is so often the case, I become so dissatisfied with what I have done as to conclude that I have undertaken a something for which I am not adapted. That I could, in any way, better solve the great problems of practical life, than they have been (if not solved, at least,) attempted heretofore, I do not, for a moment, suppose; but, if I could brush a little dust off a few soul-wings, and clear a little the perspective glass with which some are looking from the Delectable Mountains towards the City of the Great King, I should rejoice as one who has found great spoil.

"In the matter of health I have been fluctuating—very different on different days without assignable cause—varying in a greater degree than mere barometrical changes account for—but still better; and to-day is a very good day—not weak, less expectoration—not feverish—and altogether in agreeable condition. I have, indeed, a vast combination of blessing that ought to make me happy—such a full blessedness of wedded-love and home-life—so many friends who sympathise with me—the sense, on looking back, that, however ill some duties have been discharged, I cannot accuse myself of general indolence, or any wholesale waste of what I have received; and, in the very disorder itself, such a merciful freedom from pain hitherto, that I could scarcely have supposed, but from indisputable stethoscopic evidence, that so desperate a malady had laid hold on me as it has. According to my present experience, I would sooner have this as a disorder to die of, than any that could be named. I dread physical suffering more than death. I am to a certain extent engaged to write, as far as health allows, for the *British Quarterly;* but, with my present strength, I can still combine some such occasional work as that I spoke of, with the modicum I do of this. . . . I have just been reading Mrs. Browning's new poem, 'Aurora Leigh,' with great pleasure—it is quite a nineteenth century epic. My wife sends her very kind love to M— and L—, and desires to be remembered to you, as do I to Mr. K—, if still with you. How is Tom? Still keeping better, I hope. Send Mrs. H— my love, when you have a safe means of conveyance; and, finally, forget not my affectionate remembrances both to M— and L—, and my blessing to the chicks.

"Very truly your friend,

"R. A. VAUGHAN."

To his sister Octavia in India :—

"April 17, 1857.

"Westbourne Park.

"BELOVED O.,

"I am a wretch, I know, for not having written to you last mail, but somehow, not calculating the day of the month, it slipped by, and it was too late; then we meant to write by Marseilles, and that in the same way eluded us; so you may imagine what knots we both tied in our noses to make us remember. At last here goes. I do hope most ardently that the rest may set you up again after that horrid journey. I am afraid India will have its lassitude as well as England; but it should have a fair trial, and with good spirits and plentiful employment I do not see why it should not benefit you yet. The moonlights must be lovely. Books you say are plentiful. Get Carl to teach you botany, and make a herbarium of your own; you might find a little science less fatiguing and abstract than any other study. You must find the singing at church agreeable, as I am sure it must be a great acquisition to what one may call 'the colony.' I live in the quietest, most regular way, generally working in the mornings, sometimes evenings too, at writing for the 'British Quarterly,' and enjoying the same very much. I wake every morning and feel that I am going to do that day just what I should like best to do. This is my *general* feeling, and it shows one is in one's element. I have been free from suffering, and my fluctuations have not been very material. I believe myself to be making way; so I cannot be sufficiently thankful. We subscribe to Mudie's, and I belong to the London Library; so our supply of books is enormous. I perpetrated a water-colour the other day, during a week of repose after the 'British Quarterly' came out. Not going out in evenings I see very little company, and so have not much social news to tell you. . . . There are going to be grand oratorio performances at the Crystal Palace; and all the world and his wife are going to Manchester in the summer to the Art Exhibition. I do not know whether *I* and *my* wife are going. Crinoline is increasing to such an extent that it's becoming impossible to invite more than one well-dressed woman an evening to any moderate-sized house. . . .

"I suppose some missing of us in England is only natural, and these domestic separations are a vile necessity; but, even had you been in England, we should have been practically almost as much separated; and, if you had been at Manchester, you would have had much less to amuse and interest you than you have now. If you were back in England to-morrow, you would miss some things in India that must be pleasant. Avoid wishes and reveries as you would poison; fill your mind with something active, practical, or serviceable, even when your body is quiet and necessarily inactive. Don't live too internal a life, and be sure that despondency is the *devil* in your case; and, if you will follow these simple rules, you will not be at leisure to regret England so much as you tell us you do, and will find life opening round you pleasantly. God bless you.

"Your affectionate BROTHER."

During the period under review, the writer penned the following lines on the words 'Our Conversation is in Heaven,' which deserve a place here.

"Our Conversation is in Heaven."

As one who hears that some long-parted friend
Hath among strangers died, and left to him
Some far away estate—doth often send
His curious fancy and surmises dim
To that faint distant land of alien speech,
Wondering how broad his acres there may be;
Doth sail at length, and that rich island reach,
To find its wide-armed ports and flowery lea,
Its city-keys, its champaign, and its towers,
All—all are his, and he is hailed a king!
Thus, O my soul, in thy most heavenward hours,
Musing on heaven, thy best imagining
Is mean and cold to what thou soon shalt see,
When Christ from thence shall say—Now rest thou here with me!

As frozen men, within the Arctic snows,
Mimic with roofing on their ice-locked deck
An English housetop, and among the floes'
Forlornly prison'd house;—a sable speck

Mid bare and boundless whiteness ;—as they muse
On English Christmas and the hearths of home,
On all the meeting mirth and love they lose ;—
As, in the skies they watch the fiery foam
Of the wild northern lights, and think how cold
Their far-flung splendours to the joyous light
Of that long-sunken sun they loved of old ;—
So to our yearning through life's wintry night
Seems earth's delight,—so wan, so soon it flies,
Beside the home and sunshine of the skies.

There are also two letters addressed to his friend, the Rev. H. R. Reynolds of Leeds, that should be inserted in this place :—

"May 29, 1856. Clifton.

"My dear Reynolds,

"I rejoiced in receiving your letter. It was very good of you to write among the fatigues of travelling, and with doubtless a good many expectations to satisfy from those desirous of hearing from you. W—— sent me a copy of the letter you wrote to your church from the Nile. An exquisite piece of writing in a literary point of view, but it possesses far higher qualities, and was as a pleasant song to my soul; it did me good, it was deep and true. That idea of the scanty receptivity of our unbelieving hearts for the fulness of the divine blessing — in whatever form, sank into my thoughts among inward responses, and has a shrine and chapelry of its own to this hour. I hope your strength has much increased since you wrote. May you come back in vigour. I imagine your impatience to be doing something once more. But I dread preaching in East Parade Chapel for you. If you can take to the pen as a help, without having to lean on it for sustenance, do. It is true the pulpit now, more than ever, needs first-rate occupants, or the press will displace it still farther—but that duty rests with men of lungs untouched. I much long to see you. I have been here a month; have not advanced, but certainly not receded, in general strength—feel even vigorous, physically; but the extremely damp weather is against me. I pine—a prisoner of clouds and vapours—for the loving sunshine. I have been writing a historical paper, not of any research, but of generalization rather, besides reading classics in a desultory manner. My future is altogether on the lily and the sparrow footing. I never did look forward far—now less than ever. I have no dissipated day-dreams to mourn over, for I have never indulged them. I think I now reap the benefit of having always concentrated my mind on present action —working after my own standard—and leaving the future, and all the accidents of reputation, to be wrought out for me somehow. I think what I have done has realized quite as much success as it deserved, and in some respects, much more than I had ventured to anticipate. My wife cordially responds to the kind wishes transmitted by yours.

"I shall probably be here for nearly another month, unless I run up to town for a few days. I shall have the more inducement so to do if I hear that you have arrived in London. Cura ut valeas.

"Thine most truly,

"R. A. VAUGHAN."

"Aug. 30th, 1856. Harborne, Birmingham.

"MY DEAR REYNOLDS,

"I am very sorry to hear that preaching has proved too much for you. It seems much more mysterious to me that you should have been so arrested, than that I should have been laid aside. But how little do we any of us know! At least thus much we may conjecture, that when the very organs requisite for speech remain seriously affected, it cannot be designed that we should be useful by preaching—we receive as plain an intimation as any spoken words can give—do something else, I appoint you to another work—or, it may be, to simple patient resignation. However, this is not the only world in which there is active service to be done. Sometimes in depression, and when not so well as usual,

I feel as though my life were quite wound up—as though I had done all I was to do,—could not count on the life or energy requisite for any fresh undertaking—and were without any purpose or aim of interest in life. Speaking being impossible, and writing, as I would, out of the question, there seems nothing more, except to live from day to day, without looking forward a single step, doing what little I can immediately, and awaiting the future. Then again, at other times I feel as if there might be some years of life and worthy labour yet in store. I have taken a house in London, but I can scarcely conceive of myself as actively employed in a home of my own again, and in working order. I look back much more than forward, and enjoy over again the manifold mercies of a life which has been exempted from the heavier calamities of humanity. The wet weather here, in a place very beautiful but somewhat damp, has been against me; but the last two days I have felt much better; I have still more cough and expectoration than I like. My sleep is good, and strength not lessened, certainly, varying much with weather—or, at least, so I fancy. Except at the upper lobe, I think the right lung now works nearly as well as the left, a result which I can only attribute to the practice of inhaling, which I still continue.

I am delighted with your praise of my book. . . . I think there is full ground for your remarks. The necessity I felt myself under of criticising as I went along, has given more prominence to censure than praise—since the former is at once more specific and varied, from the nature of the case—while the admirable spirit of many of the mystics personally is indicated in more general terms. The result seems to me such as to induce readers to suppose me less charitable than I really am perhaps. Those who read so attentively as you, however, will perceive where the notes supplement the text, sometimes very materially. Now I must go out and enjoy the sunshine. I leave this neighbourhood early next week. . . . Pray let me hear of your plans, as far as you can form them. I should have great faith in your case in the effect of a total abstinence from any exertion of the voice; but I am afraid, where the lungs are even touched, that speaking is as though a man should insist on walking several miles a day with a gouty leg, and expect to get better under the aggravation. My wife is with me here; joins me in kind remembrances to Mrs. R., and the best wishes for yourself.

"I abide, my dear Friend,

"Most truly yours,

"ALFRED VAUGHAN."

The next letter is of a somewhat later date, and was written to an old college friend, now a clergyman, for whom my son had always cherished an affectionate esteem, but from whom he had been separated, in the course of providence, for some years past. In requesting that the autograph letter should be returned to him, Mr. Paterson says :—

"It is now one of a few, and because few, very "precious relics, of a friend whose friendship, though "of many years' duration, was never clouded by the "expression, nor, so far as I know, by the existence "of one feeling of irritation. He is gone, young in "years—but for *him* we may not lament the dispensa-"tion—for assuredly he was not only mature in intellect, "but rich in grace. I delight to think of him as one "of that 'blessed company'—the church above—to "the perfected love and friendship of some members "of which I love to look forward, if by God's grace, "I may be found worthy to attain to it."

"March 5, 1857.

"19, Alexander-street, Westbourne Park, W.

"MY DEAR PATERSON,

"I can't send you so long a letter as I should like to do, for desk-work is not good for me, and I have rather too much of it as it is. With a million things to say, I cannot but hope all the more that in some way we may see each other before the year is out. If I go to Manchester in the summer we will try. I like the picture of your blessed, useful life; mine is as quiet, though I am not doing so much good. Here, in London, as I am, I am still secluded, for I can never go out in evenings. My long morning is generally given to writing, the evenings to reading—sometimes to writing too—which is not always wise. Now and then I get haunted by what I am doing—pursued by it—and then it is time to stop. Though my disorder is of the lung, too much brain-work brings on hectic symptoms; but, considering the extent of the injury—nothing less than a considerable cavity in the upper part of the right lung—I am wonderfully well. I shall certainly be glad for you to see my book, which will tell you as well as any letters what my employments have been for the last few years. It was written in the midst of preaching, and pastoral duties of all sorts, or it would have been perhaps less fragmentary. Don't you remember what heaps of poetry I used to send you for criticism in our Shelley days? I hardly ever write a line now, yet I am happier than I was then, in spite of time, for the deep peace of domestic happiness is far above the restless ambition of youth. One source of the disquiet of youth is the being unable to make one's self out, and know what one can or cannot do. Now time interprets ourselves to us, and manhood, having accepted the interpretation, is at peace. Then, too, one gets a truer, larger view of life, and the morbid passion for distinction is elevated into a desire to do one's best in the appointed place. This is the true repose—the union of serenity and effort—as distinguished from feverish ambition on the one side, and mere artistic Goethe-like self-enjoyment on the other.

"The sermon is in one aspect a high walk of art, but, as you say (and as I found), too commonly a hurried composition. And after all it is the matter and not the style that is the main thing—meaning by style, mere graceful sentence-turning. I have been reading with much pleasure some of Archer Butler's sermons—a wonderful man for his years.

"In many respects I am but ill-qualified for the pastoral office—the practical quickness which understands, manages, comforts, instructs personally some hundreds of one's fellow-creatures, of every age, station, and variety of character,—in this work I was only to a moderate extent successful, and all I did was done by no wisdom or knowledge of mankind, or adroit discernment of character, but simply by kindness and sympathy; and important as these things are, they are by no means all—leave a great deal undone of rougher work, and are still more inadequate when associated, as in my case, with a certain shyness, deficient self-confidence, and want of conversational fluency. But in the study and among my books, 'my bosom's lord sits lightly on her throne,' and I have it all my own way of course, for real hard work is my delight. In this way, though nothing but death itself staring me in the face, as it did, would have persuaded me to relinquish my sacred duties, now that the blow has come, I cannot deny that my present occupation is very congenial to my natural tastes. And, indeed, there are plenty to supply my place.

"With our united kind regards to yourself and your wife, whom I hope I may know, and you mine, before so very long,

"I am, my dear Paterson,

"Your affectionate Friend,

"R. A. VAUGHAN."

The reader will not be insensible to the tone of subdued pathos which pervades this letter. The name of the friend to whom it was addressed had been intimately associated with the young and cheerful days of the past. The realities of the future had now come into the place of many a dream in that past. Much there was in the circumstances of the writer for which his Christian heart could be grateful—in which he could be even joyous. But in looking back to those departed years, the path was seen to be strewed with hopes and wishes, which, like faded flowers, were never to blow again. It may be well that much of the fondness of those early days should die out, but it was pleasant to have possessed it, and who can think of it as gone without emotion? In such retrospects there may be a melancholy thoughtfulness without sin. But the man had learnt something who had become convinced that happiness is best found in labour prosecuted for higher ends than mere fame on the one hand, or mere self-enjoyment on the other.

From the spring of 1857, when the above letter was written, to midsummer, my son's health could not be said to be improving, rather otherwise. In June he arranged to spend a quiet six weeks or two months in Germany, mostly in places near the Rhine. The relaxation and change seemed to be highly beneficial to him. But, on his return, evil tidings awaited him.

His eldest sister had married Dr. Carl Buch, who had become Principal of the Government College at Bareilly, in Upper India. Since Christmas, 1856, his youngest sister had been resident in that place with the eldest. Before returning from Germany he had been informed that his sisters had been sent, with other ladies, to the hills, as there was room to fear that the Sepoys at Bareilly might follow the example of the mutineers at Meerut and Delhi. Those fears were too soon realized. The Bareilly rebels spared no European that fell into their hands. Dr. Buch was reported at first as among the missing. For a time, his friends, who knew his alertness and courage, seemed confident that he must have escaped. But in August the news came that several civilians had been seized in Bareilly, and murdered, and Dr. Buch was one of these. Dr. Buch had been a student with my son in Lancashire and at Halle. The tidings concerning him, and the anxiety felt by my son as to the possible fate of his sisters, so affected him, that in the night after the day on which this shock came he had a new attack of hemorrhage. Under careful treatment even these symptoms seemed soon to subside. But the disturbance had been mischievous. It left a greater difficulty of breathing than had been hitherto experienced.

This form of ailment increased as the autumn advanced. On the morning of the 23rd of October my son suffered so much from this cause, and from pains in the side and chest, that the physician was sent for in much haste. The means used were for the time successful. During the greater part of that day, and of the following Saturday and Sunday, he seemed to be recovering. It is now known that for some time past he had been looking upon his life as not likely to be of long continuance. But his conversation on the days mentioned was for the most part cheerful, giving no indication of any sense of immediate danger. He continued in bed, but in a sitting posture, and was employed through much of both those days in reading, and even in writing.

But about seven o'clock on Monday morning the difficulty of respiration felt on Friday returned. The pain in the chest and side did not recur. The diseased lung had now become so charged that without relief in that quarter the issue threatened to be serious. No such relief could be given. About two hours after this seizure had commenced, the sufferer, on being reminded of the goodness of God, which had helped him through so much, replied, with emphasis—"Yes—God is very good." These were all but his last words. He said soon afterwards, but with much calmness of manner, "This is very like dying." The rest was silence. During the next half-hour there was often a smile on his face which spoke when the tongue could not, and the last breath passed as a gentle sigh, and all was ended. So his pure spirit came to know, according to his own words, what it is to have that last event "over;" to have "death *behind*, and not *before*," and was summoned to those regions where it becomes a matter of consciousness, and not merely of faith, that "this life is not our only sphere of action."

It is not for me to attempt an analysis or estimate of the character of the man whose career came thus to its conclusion. It will be best, I presume, that I should leave that to persons who may be expected to speak with less partiality, and in some respects from better knowledge. A letter with which I have been favoured by the Rev. H. R. Reynolds, now President of Cheshunt College, expresses in strong terms his appreciation of the mind and worth of his friend, Alfred Vaughan, and the reader has ample means of testing the truth of that gentleman's representations.

"Leeds, Feb. 1858.

"DEAR DR. VAUGHAN,

It is now fifteen years since I was first introduced to your dear son. He was at that time in the senior classes of the University College, London, but was regarded by his junior colleagues with a mixture of awe and affection. He was known then among us as a man of erudition, genius, and perseverance, but accessible and generous withal, and apparently unconscious of his own superior attainments.

"As he and I completed our curriculum at different colleges, and were subsequently settled in the ministry at a great distance from each other, our almost casual acquaintance hardly ripened into friendship until within the last five or six years. During this period some resemblance in our pursuits, and a still greater similarity in the providential discipline to which we were submitted, provoked sympathy, correspondence, and intercourse, the memory of which I shall always guard with sacred gratitude. My only reason for referring to this is, that, although I have somewhat presumptuously undertaken to pen the following lines, it was not my privilege to watch the development of his mind. I knew him best when the fruits of all he had learned, and fashioned, and felt, were ripening in the light of immortality, and God's hand was stretched out to receive them. I knew him best when all the strong and beautiful things that he had gathered in his richly-stored mind were grouped into the glorious order, which gave them fresh charm,—when he seemed to realize the bright and true form of 'la sainte indifférence' of the best of those mystics whose holiness and whose mistakes he had so delicately analysed,—when he appeared much absorbed in the grandeur of that life which he knew to be eternal, and the depth of that love which he found to be the Father's. Much that he said and wrote to me under these circumstances seemed like the footfall of the Messenger that has fetched him away from us.

"You have not required that I should touch on these subjects, and you are setting a wonderful example to those who loved and lament him—rather to study his life, than to mourn too deeply over his death. It gives me inexpressible pleasure to be permitted to bring just one stone, and lay it by his grave, believing that your hand will polish it, and put it into its rightful place.

"Since Alfred left us, I have re-read the greater portion of his published works, and looking at them in their entireness, it seems to me that his mind was cast in one of those rare moulds which the Father of our spirits does not often use, at all events I know not where to find his parallel.

"There was extraordinary individuality about his style —so that, though he published anonymously, he was almost invariably betrayed. This was not in consequence of any peculiar opinions, any crotchet, any oft-used illustrations, any singular sweep or dash of his sentences, any of that epigrammatic verbiage, or misplacement of words, or tricks, or great feats of language, by which many of his contemporaries are easily recognised. I may be somewhat blinded by the long-sustained pleasure of recent communion with his writings; but it seems to me that they contain many passages which might be fairly compared with the blaze of Ruskin, the magic of De Quincey, or with the efforts of Jeffries or Macaulay. Still there was a subtle combination of feature which he gave to his thought that was peculiarly his own. He wrote with no half-concealed bias, but had a fellow-feeling for great truths, which aided him by an instinctive exercise of all his faculties to find them wherever they were hidden, and then, 'like a fire-fly on a flower,' he made them seem more truthful by poising over them.

"Will you suffer me to enumerate a few things which may set forth what appears to me to have constituted the *individuality* by which we always recognised him?

"Perhaps that which struck every reader at a glance was

the extraordinary brilliance of his fancy and the affluence of his stores of illustration; for this gave at once the charm of an illuminated manuscript to his productions to any one who was disposed to study the by-play of his thoughts. He appeared able to lay all nature, history and life under contribution for this purpose; and he accomplished his task so easily, so freely, so naturally, that his strange similes, and often far-fetched colours, had the look of being fashioned or acted somewhere for his special behoof and advantage; yet a volume of notes might be added to his collected writings, which would afford endless amusement, and include almost encyclopædic information. There is poetry enough in his *Hours with the Mystics* to stock half-a-dozen such poets as we hear of in these days. In the big dreams of Willoughby, in the saucy frolic, the bursting wit, and marvellous eloquence of what he, in his editorial capacity, called 'the distressing outbreaks of Gower,' one feels disposed to say, 'This man was meant for a poet, not a philosopher.' It will be acknowledged, however, by all, that in his later writings especially, his ample illustrations do not burden his ideas, and never really distract attention from his theme. On the contrary, even when he rose to the dignity of imaginative narrative, he still left his moral purpose more distinctly impressed upon the mind of his reader than any of the clothing in which he decked it.

"To my mind, your son's *power of analysis* was as remarkable as the stores of his fancy were vast; and as Atherton is to Gower, so is the clear definition to the brilliant image; so is the acute division of metaphysical subtleties or the logical sequence of his thoughts, to the startling or gorgeous illustration. I remember in his article on 'Origen,' while undertaking to explain to some extent the harmonizing principles in some of the divergent opinions of that great man, he affects to long 'for the shrewdness of a certain naturalist who had discovered a close analogy between pigs and humming-birds.' Whether this would have availed him matters not; he did possess the rare power of analyzing opinions, and discovering their constituents, of classifying their common elements, of tracing them through many diverse manifestations, and of reasoning with great persuasiveness and robust energy.

"Instances of these characteristics might be produced in great numbers; such, for example, as his classification of mysticism in his opening chapters; his review in a note of the five different combinations of Platonism with Christianity; his luminous comparison of the 'reminiscence' of the Platonists with the 'ecstasy' of the Neo-Platonists, and his mode of indicating the relation of Tauler to Eckart, or of Emerson to the Persian Sufis. Indeed, analytical power of high order distinguishes all his writings.

"Now, poetry and analysis, though very often disjoined from each other, or impeding one another's exercise, have not unfrequently been combined in our greatest writers. Your son added to this combination *rare and accurate erudition.* His acquaintance with the languages of ancient and modern Europe, with Dutch and Spanish, as well as awkward Greek and defunct German; his classical feeling, and his power of throwing himself back fully into the times whose mental efforts and diseases he prepared himself to chronicle, gave him great advantage; and so we find him, with almost equal ease, composing a letter for Philo and an oration for Ammonius Saccas, sermons for Tauler and conversations between him and Ruysbroeck, visions for Suso and dreams for Santa Theresa; but verifying every sentence by authorities, and often (as I have had occasion to find) condensing into a clear and ringing line the spirit of a dusty folio-page, originally written in the crabbed archaic dialect of a foreign tongue. The extensive acquaintance he possessed with the literature of Europe excites wonder as to the means by which he could possibly have acquired so much, the joy that he used his stores so felicitously, and the regret that God did not permit him to bring more of his treasures into this earthly temple of His glory.

"After all, the real combining factor in his mental constitution, and which made him so clearly *himself*, was something more and better than either *poetry*, or *analysis*, or *erudition;* it was his manifest and irrepressible *love of truth.* The truth that he loved was truth given to us rather than excogitated by us; and in virtue of this love he appears, in my humble judgment, to have thrown needed light on the relation of revelation to philosophy.

"In reviewing so many of those phases and diseases of thought which verged on, or were developed into, genuine mysticism, and further, in his articles on 'Origen,' 'Schleiermacher,' 'Hypatia,' 'Dr. Tauler,' 'Madam Guion,' and the 'Theologia Germanica,' as well as in his truly great work *Hours with the Mystics*, he had a delicate task to fulfil, for he was treading on that border region between philosophy and inspiration, wherein, if anywhere besides in God's Book, the mind of the present generation is disposed to look for the analogue, if not the example, of genuine inspiration. Your son traversed the whole country, and, without conceding an iota of his exclusive deference to the inspirations of Scripture, or arrogantly condemning the strong convictions of his clients, he produces an accumulative and resistless argument against the vague claims of any fictitious faculty or semi-supernatural abstraction of the soul, to rise above, or do without, the religion of evidence, of proved fact, of demonstrated and felt appropriateness. He shows how mysticism in all its forms, in trying to 'soar above means, experience, history, and external revelation, ends by mistaking a hazy reflex of its own image for the Deity.' He has written for us the whole history of the process by which a 'night fell on reason, imagination, memory, and on all our real powers, that an imaginary power might awake,—and he has shown how this process was repeated so often, that though (to take one of his own profound remarks) 'mysticism has no genealogy,' we see that power at work in every degree of approximation to the faith of Christ, and he gives us the means of combating it in every place. He has worked out the following principle as a counter-action, that wherever 'we accept on faith statements which are as yet unexplained, we do so on grounds which the understanding shows to be sound.' Yet at the same time he has with loving and reverent hand followed the principal conclusions of the mediæval mystics, and revealed the beneficent and even reforming tendency of the truth that was in them, separating the chaff from the wheat, and garnering the good seed for our use. Nor did he under-estimate the strength of those convictions which are created by a complex of all the spiritual powers of man's soul, nor fail to observe that the logical faculty cannot always analyse the intensity of the thoughts which the spiritual man espouses and lives by. In his article on Dr. Tauler, he has sketched with master hand the theology of the precursors of the Reformation, and shown with reverent care, that the noblest of the mystics were saved from utter Pantheism by their faith in the Christ of History.

"His philosophy acutely defines its own limits, and ever leads him with open arms to receive God's truth, rather than his own. The scope of his task not only allowed him to do this much for the exhibition of the true Divine informant of man, but brought him continually face to face with the actual truths of God's revelation, in their points of contrast with the virtual substitutes which have been proffered. Thus, for instance, he has shown most satisfactorily that an attempt to do without the *human* nature of Christ soon takes THE CHRIST away from us, and that to evade the law of our minds by which we need the external presentation to us of God in man, ends in substituting the mind's creation for the Creator. He often had occasion in spirit to urge that, whatever system of philosophy renders an 'appeal to others impossible,' confers 'on conscientious differences the authority of conflicting inspirations.' His work is a demonstration of the fact that, if 'know thyself' is to be interpreted to mean 'find in thyself an infallible repertory of needed truth,'—it is replete with all the monstrosities of idolatry. He is led on to show that any attempt of humanity to produce out of the depths of its own consciousness a Christ and to establish a claim for the Evangelists out of *their* correspondence with that ideal, is consequently absurd; as though German doctors could have spun a Christ out of their profundities, if it had not been for the fishermen of Galilee.

"I have already expanded this letter to unreasonable limits, or I might most easily have shown the method in which he dealt with the great doctrines of God, of sin, and of redemption. At every point he was in close quarters, not with denials of these great revelations of Scripture, but with the way in which enthusiasm aped them, or philosophy thought it had solved their mysteries, or folly ignored their special significance, or travestied their momentous import;—but I forbear.

"It would have been a pleasing task to have presented a catena of glorious passages—a whole harvest of genial touches, and long lists of rememberable sayings; but this is unnecessary. He rose into eminence at a bound. His genius is as rare as his labour must have been excessive; the bent of his whole mind as reverent as his flight was soaring.

"I had occasion to know how kind and generous he was; how willing to guide, how competent to teach, and how ready with his stores of information. These stores were not shut up in notebooks, but always at hand; nor did he seem to have any idea how really great he was. No one who knew him could choose but love him; and when he reciprocated that love, it was like the sunshine and showers of heaven. He is in the Father's house, and we would not have him now away from his home.

"I am, dear Dr. Vaughan,

"With much respect and sympathy, yours most truly,

"H. R. REYNOLDS."

Mr. Reynolds has kindly favoured me with the following postscript to his letter.

"Cheshunt College, December, 1863.

"Nearly six years have elapsed since you kindly permitted me to furnish a few remarks for insertion in the sketch of your son's life. I am thankful for the present opportunity of reviewing the estimate which I then ventured to give of his intellectual powers, and for the privilege of adding a few lines on the impression produced upon me by his beautiful life and ways. I am not conscious of creating an ideal of mental and moral excellence and then calling it 'Alfred Vaughan;' yet I am sure I might be charged with such an offence if I were to write all that I now feel. It is easy to be mistaken, yet I imagine that I know him now more truly than it was possible for me to do when he first was snatched away from earthly work and love. He was *great*, and at this distance it is easier to comprehend the whole outline of his work and life than when the opened grave that yawned between us seemed so wide, and the first effort to understand the vision that had passed away was weakened by the sorrow of the parting.

"Some flowers laid up in the folded leaves of a book retain their beauty and fragrance, and recall, when opened upon, the associations in which they were first plucked—so now your kind permission to add a postscript to my letter, brings back some of the rememberable hours which he and I passed together.

"My letter described points and peculiarities of his mental constitution and character; the prominent thought which now possesses me is, that of the completeness and harmony of these with his whole life. The symmetry of his being—like the proportions of some world-famous temples—almost detracts from the magnitude of his separate faculties and aims. He was, he must have been, conscious of his superiority to most of those with whom he came into contact, because every day he lived and every effort that he made showed him that he moved freely through regions of thought where many of his compeers toiled and panted with ill-disguised effort: yet he wielded his various and ponderous acquisition with such lightness, dexterity, and grace, that he always gave me the impression of profound modesty and humility. This impression was often created by the discovery that in conversation and correspondence he was selecting a few only out of his many reasons for opinions which he had formed, that he held back a reserve of illustrations and proofs equally apt and convincing. He would, at the same time, defer to, and weigh the arguments of others, when they were offered on grounds which were narrow and meagre compared with his own ample stores of information and thought.

"He had, moreover, an eye for excellence, and beauty, and truth everywhere, and this made him singularly impartial in his criticisms, lenient where some others were hastily severe, and constantly alive to the points and degrees where he fancied and urged that others surpassed him. He said and wrote disparaging things about himself, and his modesty did more than temper his ambition.

"It was impossible to enjoy anything like familiar intercourse with your beloved son, without being made joyous by his mirthfulness and unrestrained humour. There was nothing caustic in his fun, but it was a merry peal of gladness which would hide the absurd in an antagonist under an extinguisher of smiles and laughter. I never heard him say an unkind or ungenerous thing, nor wither by a sarcasm that which he could not overcome by an argument. His perception of the ludicrous was keen, and his wit sparkled like dewdrops on the flowers: and so he shed a charm over common things, and 'added sunshine to daylight, making happy things happier.'

"I have been told how, when occasion arose for it, he

was severe in his reprimand of wrong, and combined firmness and gentleness with such marvellous tact, as to melt the wrong doer into confession and contrition.

"Nothing was more obvious in him than the generous and warm affection which he manifested for those whom he loved. He saw them in the colours in which his love enshrined them, and lent to them and their doings some of the hues fresh borrowed from his own heart. At the ordination of his brother-in-law in Halifax,—one who has since followed him to his home,—he spoke with such manly tenderness of their college friendship, and their brotherly love, that it seemed even then and there to be stretching out into the everlasting bliss in which the two brothers are now united. The way in which he spoke and wrote to me of some extreme physical suffering of the one who was dearest to him, even months after the event, showed that his sensitive nature was still vibrating with the thrill of that earnest sympathy.

"As he drew nearer to the great awakening, the veil that hides all from our gaze became almost translucent. He never seemed to fear or doubt, and strangely expressive words and thoughts fell from his lips. He once spoke to me with a kind of joyousness of the fact, that he had tested life at so many points that he did not imagine that it was possible for him to receive fundamentally different ideas of its mystery and of its meaning. 'The circumference of life may widen,' said he, 'with every new phase and change of work, but every new experience must prove, on this side the grave, a repetition, an expansion and improvement of older experience, and not a fresh revelation. Knowledge may prove an ever-broadening circle, but it will be always confined to one plane.' He seemed to think that this was a premonition of the hour when he should be admitted to the glorious liberty of the sons of God, and be full of light, having no part dark. He more than once spoke to me of death as a perplexing and anxious event in the eternal life of which he seemed to be intensely conscious, and said, with a marvellous emphasis, 'It will be grand to get death well over.'

"On another occasion, he said to me, 'The love of father, and mother, and wife, and child, and friend are all but infinitely strong, but, after all, these earthly affections can only be faint shadows of the divine love.' I never knew a man who seemed more 'alive unto God through Jesus Christ our Lord' than he.

"It is unusual to meet with one who, at such an early age, has completed a noble life, and been cultured by the Holy Spirit to such a harmony of intellectual and spiritual character, inspiring almost equal reverence for the subtlety and force of his mental energies and the holiness and beauty of his moral and religious life. The memory of his friendship some of us guard as a precious treasure; but the world outside can only dimly guess what THEY have lost who could call him—Son, Husband, or Father."

It will be remembered that my son's connexion with Birmingham extended from 1850 to 1855. During a large portion of that interval the Rev. J. B. Paton, now Theological Tutor in the Congregational Institute in Nottingham, was resident near that town, and had ample opportunity of knowing the subject of this *Memoir* both in his private and public relations. I know of no one else to whom I could so well look to give me a satisfactory estimate of my son's position as a preacher.

"DEAR SIR,

"I thank you for allowing me to inform others who are interested in the life of your lamented son, of some of his characteristics as a student and Christian minister, that so they may know him better, whom I esteem it the highest privilege to have known and loved during the last six years of his life. I will restrain every expression of that sorrowful feeling which this task has profoundly revived, though I can only pourtray, however imperfectly, his character as it is now mirrored and preserved in the liveliest affections of my soul. In order to condense my letter, and to set forth most clearly such facts concerning my beloved friend as may be most interesting, I shall speak of him as a preacher, a theologian, and a Christian.

"While a student in Spring-hill College, it was my privilege to attend his ministry for three years, and to hear him as often as my own preaching engagements would allow. I speak not only for myself, but for some others of my fellow-students, when I thankfully acknowledge how much our spiritual life was deepened and quickened by his ministrations of Divine truth. His style of preaching became somewhat altered during these three years, in that he left the more abstruse themes to which his researches as a student often conducted him, and confined himself to the exposition of those grand spiritual truths which were the strength and joy of his own soul, and bore at once upon the religious life of his hearers. In proportion as he drew less from the material of his study, and more from the religious spirit in which he directed his studies, he came nearer to the hearts of his hearers, and spoke to them with greater directness and unction, and awoke gently but irresistibly their holiest feelings by the unaffected earnestness of his own. His sermons during this time gradually partook of a beautiful simplicity and intense spirituality, which adapted them to all classes of his hearers, and clothed them with a quiet but thrilling power, such as I have never felt to attend another preacher.

"Recalling the hallowed impressions of these sermons, the memory of which yet lingers with me like that of some Divine melody, I would state briefly some of the causes of that marvellous effect which I know resulted in other cases beside my own, from some of his sublimely simple discourses.

"In preparation for the pulpit, he adopted what must be the happiest and most useful method when there is a fluent and ready command of language—that of only arranging the order of his thoughts. This preparation, however, was carefully made, and extended to the most minute subdivisions of his plan, and to the most careful selection of illustrations and appropriate phrases. Yet he was unshackled from the burden of repeating a composition, the zest of which had passed away in the writing. The energy of his mind was spent in securing the great points of a sermon—perfection of the plan, even in its details, and richly varied, luminous illustration; while in delivery there was the vivacity of a mind earnestly engaged in communicating by a present living impulse the thoughts over which it had so carefully brooded. For this style of preaching he had uncommon qualifications. His language was abundant and exquisitely choice. They who read his works need not be informed of this. Yet often in speaking, whether it was because it was set off by the grace of his manner or not, there seemed a fulness and rhythmical sweetness in his language, which even the finest passages of his writings scarcely evince. Doubtless, much of the charm of his preaching arose from the simple and almost magical way in which the fullest and noblest words came to clothe and beautify his thoughts. Sentence after sentence fell from his lips clear and lustrous as crystal, revealing his thoughts in vivid distinctness, and riveting the attention of his hearers by their purity and compact energy. His manner was singularly quiet; one finger of the right hand occasionally extended, and moving with the rise and fall of successive sentences, being almost the only action in which he indulged. Neither did his voice rise and swell under deep passionate excitement. Not that his preaching was devoid of feeling, but his feelings seldom, if ever, in the pulpit, grew to the vehemence of passion.

"Gentle and solemn pathos was the prevailing element of his discourses. His sympathies attached him to those themes which were congenial to his modes of feeling—love, pity, sorrow; and in his expression of these he touched at will, with a light or powerful hand, the hearts of all who heard him. Though his manner was so quiet, his power over an audience was indescribable in awakening pathetic emotions. The ballad-like simplicity of his language, the tones of his voice, and the changing expressions of his face, all showed the intense reality of his own feelings, and hence readily communicated them to others. He wanted the stern and stormy temper of the δεινότης, which is supposed to be essential to an orator, but there was a spell in his gentle and natural manner which was as powerful as the most vehement passion, and produced, as do the soft dews of morning and tempered light of day, the most healthful results. His preaching was distinguished by the abundant and happy use of imagery. Often his sermons were a series of pictures; but like his Lord's, his pictures were all brilliant with the light of heaven. Nature and life became transfigured as they were seen to reveal not only the physical but the spiritual laws of God. How often I have heard him, and his expressions yet dwell with me, thrill the heart by a home picture, in which the love of the child, and the yearning care of the parent, were made to typify the Divine relations of God's family. This imagery might have been excessive and wearisome, but for the artlessness and beauty of the language in which it was drawn. I have known no one who in this respect so followed the Great Teacher, whose sermons unveil the hidden things of earth and humanity, that we may see everywhere the kingdom of God which he preached, and whose language is Divine in its perfect simplicity.

"Those who heard Mr. Vaughan will remember yet

one other characteristic which could never be forgotten by those who saw him: I refer to the pure and often seraphic expression of his countenance. When lit up with the ecstasy of holy feeling which his subject enkindled, his face shone with an effulgent light which awed me with its unearthly beauty. They who heard him preach his sermon on John iii. and second verse,—'Beloved, now are we the sons of God, and it doth not yet appear what we shall be; but we know that, when He shall appear, we shall be like Him; for we shall see Him as He is'—they will remember the transcendent power with which every person in the congregation was entranced, not only by the words of his mouth, but by the unspeakable love and faith that were shadowed on his countenance.

"As a theologian, it is not difficult to ascertain his views from his writings; but it may be necessary to show the rigid watchfulness with which he guarded himself against those theological errors to which his peculiar temperament made him prone. This is the more needful now, because many, whose natures are like his, have rushed unthinkingly into those fallacies the snare of which he carefully avoided.

"The two classes of mind broadly distinguished as the poetic and the logical must ever exist, and traverse with their differences the world of thought, the extreme of each constituting its opposite poles. The one class, by an instinctive sympathy, seeks out the resemblances that underlie things seemingly different, and presses toward that Highest Principle into which all things may be resolved. The other class marks off, and tenaciously defends, the distinctions that differentiate each individual person and thing. They, therefore, relate to each other as the centripetal and centrifugal forces of the mental world, and in their co-operation hold it in 'the mean' of its proper course. In theology these two tendencies of thought have been most conspicuously developed. Some men of catholic nature, seeking after the essential truth of religion, treat slightingly, or altogether ignore, the separate forms in which it may subsist. They anxiously exhibit the unity among different sects of Christians, and, in doing so, fritter away, as mere trifles their distinctive creeds and institutions; while others, exalting these differences as the shibboleth of their party, and spending their utmost energy in their defence, overlook and ignore the common basis of the Christian faith. In no age have these opposite tendencies been pushed into more uncontrolled excess than in ours. Every one who knew my dear friend knows that by nature he belonged to the former class. His broad catholic sympathies brought him *en rapport* with whatever truth or excellence might be possessed by any party. His logical instinct was not so apt to seize upon their inconsistencies, nor did it necessitate to his own mind a clear systematized formula of the truth which he believed, and by which all others should be tried.

"His sympathy with mysticism, which attracted him to that subject, sufficiently proves this to be the bent of his mind. Yet it is remarkable with what exactitude his sympathies are controlled by his judgment. Against his nature, he cultivated and matured his logical faculty, so that while he acknowledged and venerated whatever was good and true in these mystical doctrines, he was not carried away by that love to a blind acceptance of them. In analysis he was expert in the detection of truth, and decided on the rejection of the falsehood which was curiously inwrought with it.

"He was profoundly convinced that since no substance or essence can exist without form, so neither can any essential truth be really known, unless the formal declaration and embodiment of it be correct. Unless there be this logical completeness, even in detail—for such is the necessity of logic in the presentment of truth —it is only imperfectly known, error is mixed up with it; and hence its moral effects are either diminished or infamously distorted. Often, in conversation with him, has he expressed to me the difficulty he has felt in demanding, as it were, this exact doctrinal statement of his own beliefs, and in applying the test of formal consistency to the doctrines of others. I consider his work on Mysticism to be unexampled from the rigour with which one whose entire soul so plainly accorded with the spirit of Tauler and the nobler mystics, has balanced their creed and exposed its deficiencies. In this work, he set himself a task which disciplined the faculty that he confessed to be his weakest, and so perfectly has he done this that I know not another writer who unites such breadth of sympathy with such a correct and firmly pronounced judgment. From this tendency of his nature my friend was drawn to the study of religious history, in preference to dogmatic or abstract theology. He liked better to mingle with men, and to watch the influence of religion on their conduct, than to define terms and construct creeds, though he confessed the absolute need of the latter study as well as the former. Accordingly Church history was the favourite home of his thoughts, and he purposed his *Hours with the Mystics* to be only a preparatory 'study' for a complete History of the Christian religion. To this *magnum opus* his whole energies would have been devoted, had he been spared; and we may faintly imagine from this first effort, a work crowded with recondite information, yet living with the intense interest of a drama, what his grander and later work would have been. That dream which once fired his aspirations, and which, if realized, would have been a sublime monument of his genius, and learning, and piety, has passed away, nor is there one left who can lift his pen to fulfil his plans. He possessed one eminent qualification for his self-appointed task as a religious historian, in his vigorous imagination, which placed him instantly in the scenes and among the men of whom he was reading. This quickness and clearness of fancy gave extreme rapidity to all his mental movements, and also strengthened his memory from the distinctness with which its images were imprinted on his mind. It was this faculty re-producing the past as a present reality, exciting his feelings, and impressing his memory by the vividness of his representations, which enabled him to accumulate his materials with such tact and speed, and to condense them in the bright and breathing pictures of his book. What might we not have expected if the same disciplined powers had engaged in the sublime work of picturing the entire history of Christianity?

"I cannot here portray the private character of my friend; and if I were to do so, I might be charged with representing an ideal and not a real character. So, at any rate, I should have judged Mr. Vaughan's character, had I merely met with it in a description, and not enjoyed the felicity of knowing it by long and intimate intercourse. As regards intellectual power, his books are a true reflex of that exhaustless memory, genial humour, and brilliant imagination, which shone in his conversation as well as in his writings. But there was a spontaneity and alertness in his turns of thought and *naïve* illustrations when engaged in conversation, which exceedingly enhanced their effect. There was no satire, because there was no bitterness in his nature, but humour —quaint, fantastic, happy humour, like Paul Richter's, only more elegant—overflowed his table-talk, and imparted to it the richest flavour. Yet over all his speech and manner there breathed a sacred tenderness, which flowed not from any earthly source, but was the fragrance of a heavenly spirit. The domestic love that shone in his home, and was the bright atmosphere in which his nature bloomed, was exquisitely pure and happy. The fond joyousness, the quiet playful humour, the soft brooding Godly care, with which he delighted himself in his children, and bound their hearts to his; and, especially, the noble grace, the ceaseless courtship with which he won every day more closely to himself her whom he loved to call, 'The Angel in the House,'—here the innate manhood of Alfred Vaughan beamed upon me, the highest image I had ever dreamed of, self-forgetting, ever-thoughtful, winning, helping, hallowing affections. His wife was the presence of his heart, the companion of his highest purposes, the intimate of his studies, the one friend whose soul dwelt in his. But the concord and sympathetic oneness, the truth and ever binding nearness of this married love, was the print again of that religion which made both one in Christ. Here, as in all else, my friend's child-like faith in God gave the secret and sweetest charm to his life. His nature, which was trustful, affectionate, and given to meditation, seemed to be ground well prepared for the seed of God; and surely in it that seed so grew and fructified as is rarely seen on earth. He always appeared to me like the beloved apostle, whose head lay confidingly on the breast of Christ, and to whom were revealed the most glorious visions of the Beautiful Future of Christ's Church. The purity of conscience and womanly gentleness of feeling, the enchanting imagination and spiritual insight, the strong trust and ecstatic joy, which are especially attributed to that apostle, were all of them characteristic of my dear friend.

"His religious zeal did not indeed take the form of intense practical activity. From physical weakness, and from a feeling of inaptitude fostered by his studious habits, he shrank from that conflict with men which public labour necessarily involves. But his zeal was none the less true. It was the mighty impulse that sustained him in his literary undertakings, and it never failed him. He was persuaded that his study was the proper sphere of his labour for Christ and the Church. The delights of religious meditation were to him infinitely sweet. He loved to bring Christ near to him, and to live, even as St. John would have done, with the assurance that his dearest friend and brother was never absent from him. The one religious theme which engrossed our conversation more than any other was the Brotherhood of Immanuel. To know him as possessing the power and wisdom of God, yet as being our elder brother, was the joy of his soul. To grow up into His likeness was his single desire. And to be with Him, as now he is, in His Father's home, was his abiding hope. To recall these conversations, held through so many years, imparts a joy unspeakable and full of glory, for his child-like faith, his devoutness, his ardent longings after Christ, are the pledges I hold that now his desire and hope are fulfilled—that he is like unto Him, for He sees Him as He is. I mourn that our fellowship has been suspended. May it be renewed when we both shall see and worship Him for ever, who united our hearts on earth.

"I am, yours respectfully,

"J. B. PATON.'

"The Rev. Dr. Vaughan."

The malady which came upon my son, and the issue of it as now known, have tended to cast an air of sadness over his history. But it would be a great mistake to suppose that his life was a melancholy one. His heart was too susceptible of gratitude, and accessible to enjoyment in too many forms, to allow of that as possible. He knew more of the lighter literature of our own time, and of past time, than most men who account themselves reading men, and who read scarcely anything beside. To the frequent defects of such literature, both in principle and tendency, he was fully alive. But he knew how to separate the chaff from the wheat, and that it belongs to genius to be often suggestive and instructive in ways which it does not itself contemplate. The gift itself he regarded as eminently divine. He deplored its abuses—but of its uses, whether tending to laughter or to tears, he was religiously observant. It was natural that such a man should have his alternations of feeling; but in general his reflective habits were no more inconsistent with a genuine cheerfulness, than his exquisite sensibility was inconsistent with a real courage. In domestic and social intercourse his manner was characterised by a buoyancy, humour, and geniality which often seemed to take every one along with him. And with regard to courage—in so far as anything personal was concerned, he scarcely seemed to know what fear was. His writings, if I mistake not, while indicating so much seriousness and tenderness of feeling, are expressive of as much vivacity and manliness of temper as was compatible with good taste. He had so little fondness for strife, that he certainly would not have committed himself to any broil about matters which seemed to him of small importance. But the thought of shrinking from consequences where great interests were at stake, was no thought to find entertainment for a moment in his breast. His habitual avoidance of every approach towards dogmatism, might lead some men to reckon upon him as a person not difficult to manage. But if the management was meant to make him a party to anything not in the strictest sense becoming, such wise persons were soon made aware of their mistake, and the rebuke administered would not be the less felt from its being tinctured probably with humour quite as much as with resentment. In truth, he rarely seemed to be more at home than when attempting to show knaves that they were by no means so clever as they imagined. In a letter for which I was indebted to my old and valued friend, Sir James Stephen, there is a reference to that 'keen eye for the comedy of life,' which betrayed itself so often in my son's conversation.

But on this point, and some others, I am happy to allow Sir James to speak for himself.

" . . . My intercourse with your son was infrequent, and I being an older man than his father, he always when we met chose rather to listen than to speak, and to give me transient glimpses into the wakings of his mind, instead of making any exhibition of them. If I had not read his poetry, his reviews (or some of them), and his *Hours with the Mystics*, I should hardly have been aware of all that was meant by the few, the simple, and the modest terms in which he was accustomed to address me. But from his writings and his conversation, illustrating each other (to his preaching I never happened to listen), I inferred that the bright-eyed, intelligent, and picturesque-looking boy, whom I had so often seen immediately below your pulpit at Kensington, had grown up just to the very bloom of early manhood, rich in a large store of accurate and well-digested scholarship, with rather a keen eye for the comedy of life, and with a taste which was gaining the mastery over that kind of luxuriance of fancy which so often attends the youth of those whom nature has marked out for future eminence.

"I shall never forget the good-humoured archness with which he accepted my protest against some of the embellishments of his book on Mysticism, nor the cordiality with which he received my suggestions for giving a greater unity of design to his future literary labours. He was one of those wise men who welcome even an unfavourable criticism when pronounced in sincerity and good faith, and on whom not even the most insignificant kindness is ever thrown away. If it had pleased God to prolong his life, it is my firm conviction that he would have accomplished the wish which I think I have more than once expressed to you regarding that branch of the Christian Church of which both he and you were ministers—the wish, I mean, that there might arise among you some men, who, in the loftiness and depth and compass of their inquiries, theological and philosophical, should forget that they were dissenters from any other religious communion, and should constrain their readers and their hearers to forget it too. He seemed to me formed to add another name to those of the great Nonconformists of the seventeenth and nineteenth centuries, and to throw over whatever he might undertake not a little of that more elaborate polish which the scholars of Oxford and Cambridge have been accustomed to regard as their peculiar boast.

"That so frequent disappointment, by a premature death, of such hopes as these, which seems to be a kind of habit in the providential government of the world, is doubtless prompted by reasons as just and profound as to us they are obscure. It remains for us all to adore them in silent acquiescence. For those to whom these mysterious dispensations bring some of the keenest of human sorrows, is reserved a far more arduous duty —the duty of meek resignation, which I think is imposed more often on the ministers of the Gospel than on other men, that they may learn by their own bitter experience a lesson which it so often falls to their lot to teach. Ever, my dear Dr. Vaughan,

"Most truly yours,

"JAMES STEPHEN."

It is even so. Minds often come into this world to raise expectations which the providence that sent them has determined shall not be realized. But in the history of that providence, much of the seemingly unwise will no doubt prove to have been only some of the profounder forms of the wise. When a mind of much penetration and fervent piety has laboured long in the track of religious thought, and comes to say—'I am tired of trying to know, seeing how little we *can* know,' it may be that the time has come when the imperfect web of the present should be woven into the richer web of the future. Certainly, what pertains to those who are left when such natures are taken should be very plain. Is it not that they should be at their work—careful that their own summons, whether coming soon or late, shall find them THERE?

The year after the decease of my son, I published a collection of his Essays, with a Memoir. A copy of that publication I sent to Sir James Stephen, which he acknowledged in the following terms:—

"April 20th, 1858.

"MY DEAR DR. VAUGHAN,

"Many thanks for the copy you have sent me of the Memoir, &c. I have been reading the two volumes with more than usual deliberation; but I find it difficult to say to you exactly what is the impression they have left upon my mind. Perhaps they have most moved me to wonder; to wonder, I mean, at my own failure, in times past, rightly to appreciate him, so that when I recall what passed at my interviews with him in his illness, I hardly know how he came to be so tolerant of my talk, or how I (even with all the apologies of age) could take upon me to discourse so copiously to such a man, and scarcely to exact of him an answer. It is little to say that he had attained an intellectual stature to which it behoved *me* to be looking upwards. Very few men indeed of his time stood on his level. His mind was so rich; his spirit so expanding to embrace whatever was praiseworthy, and so hearty to do battle with whatever was base and false; his range of thought so widely extended, and the play of his fancy, range where he might, so brilliant and so ceaseless, that I hardly know to what he might not have been equal, if it had been the good pleasure of God that his services should be rendered during a long life in this world. I see very few persons at present, but from the conversation of those whom I do meet (Milman, the Dean of St. Paul's per example), I infer that the world at large will be much of the same opinion. The one unwelcome criticism I anticipate, is that in several of his papers, the jewellery, rich and genuine as it is, has been scattered with a profusion which, with an unkind judge, may pass for ostentation. That it is poured out more lavishly than a taste severely correct would authorize, I am myself disposed to think; but, if I remember right, there is a greater restraint exercised in the 'Mystics;' and the fault, if fault it really be, was that of youth, and a fault which few indeed could have ever committed.

"What I would chiefly wish to see added to these volumes in any future edition is a little more theology, of which in the shape of sermons, or notes for sermons, one would suppose there must be a large store left. It is not that to myself the Divine and the minister of the Gospel is hidden beneath the literary and philosophical and poetical draperies in which the portrait is exhibited (for I think that the constant presence to his mind of the great practical business of his existence is evident enough), but I am not equally clear that others will find the veil as transparent as I do, and I would not have any honest man repelled from reading and delighting in what is published by any disappointment about what is not published.

"But after reading these volumes, and understanding better than before the extent of your loss, I am unable to say one word to that purpose. Time, and the energetic use of time will indeed steal away the bitterness even of such a sorrow; but I dare not hope, indeed, I hardly wish, that such a wound should ever be thoroughly healed, except by the reunion to which you are looking forward, and by the soothing influence which the prospect of that reunion will exercise over the steps conducting you towards it, even, if among them, some should be dark and painful.

"Ever yours,

"JAMES STEPHEN."

With the insertion of this letter, I take my leave of this theme. What I have felt in traversing this ground anew may be in part imagined. But God is just—just and good.

CPSIA information can be obtained
at www.ICGtesting.com
Printed in the USA
LVHW100028190422
716387LV00030B/197

9 783752 592511